SUSANNA COVERS THE CATWALK

ALSO BY MARY HOGAN:
Susanna Sees Stars
Susanna Hits Hollywood
Pretty Face
The Serious Kiss

MARY HOGAN

SUSANNA COVERS THE CATWALK

SIMON AND SCHUSTER

SIMON AND SCHUSTER
First published in Great Britain in 2008
by Simon & Schuster UK Ltd
A CBS COMPANY

1 3 5 7 9 10 8 6 4 2

Simon & Schuster UK Ltd
1st Floor
222 Gray's Inn Road
London WC1X 8HB

A CIP catalogue record for this book is
available from the British Library.

ISBN: 978-1-41690-159-4

Set in 12/17.75 pt Adobe Garamond by
Rowland Phototypesetting Ltd, Bury St Edmunds, Suffolk
Printed and bound in Great Britain by
CPI Cox and Wyman, Reading, Berkshire RG1 8EX

TO MY SISTER, DIANE. A TRUE FASHIONISTA.

ACKNOWLEDGEMENTS

This series has had a series of editors due to maternity leave and relocation. My deepest thanks go out to all of them: Venetia Gosling, Joanna Moult and the newest member of the Susanna team, Jenny Glencross. Each one of you has contributed to making Susanna the gutsy girl she is. Thank you! A Prada handbag full of gratitude to the Press Office of Olympus Fashion Week in New York for letting me peer behind the velvet ropes . . . even though neither one of us knew what I might see. Much love to my awesome agent, Laura Langlie. (I've run out of adjectives!) And, as always, a gazillion kisses to my husband Bob who is my first reader and biggest fan.

ONE

I never dreamed it would happen to me. I've become a fashionista.

'A fasha*what*?' Dad asked me when I told him that Nell Wickham, *Scene* magazine's uber-glam editor, had offered me the chance to cover New York's major style event: Fashion Week.

'A couture cognoscenti,' I informed him, having just memorised the term.

'I see,' he said, though he didn't see at all. Not that it mattered. Fashionistas like *moi* aren't into labels – except designer ones, of course. And, FYI, we have our very own language which uses foreign words like *moi* and *cognoscenti* and abbreviations like FYI.

Becoming a fashionista is one of the hardest things I've ever done. Mostly because I had so many *other* things to do, like cram for my killer finals at the end of sophomore year, spend the summer doing community service (my school adviser flat-out refused to consider last summer's catering to Nell Wickham's every neurotic need as *service*. Can you believe it??), and start a new school year in which I, Susanna Barringer, am determined to get a bonafide boyfriend. My fantasy relationship with Hollywood mega-hottie Randall Sanders is over. It's time to get real.

So, in every spare moment I've had for the past six months, I've been studying style. I watched *Project Runway* and *Full Frontal Fashion* on television. I devoured *Vogue*. While babysitting my three baby brothers – two-and-a-half-year-old triplets – I practised speaking Fashionese.

'Henry, your Boyz in the Hoodie sweatshirt and cargo pants are too matchy-matchy,' I said.

'I wuv Elmo,' he replied.

My Fashion Immersion has taught me that grey is the new black, shorts are the new trousers, long sweaters are the new shirts. Round-toe shoes are *in*; balloon-poppers are *out*. Or, is pink the new grey? Are trousers the new shorts? Is a waistcoat the new sweater? Honestly, it's impossible to know for sure because, when it comes to fashion, there's only one rule that's set in stone: the moment a trend is solidified, designers will trip over themselves to change it.

So, for the past few months, my brain has been over-heated with fashion temperatures: cool looks, hot trends, white-hot accessories. I learned the difference between a 'catwalk' and a 'runway'. A catwalk is an *elevated* pathway for a model to strut her stuff; a runway is on the ground. But few fashionistas get that technical. Unless, of course, they're talking about an empire bodice, which is the new waistline. Or, is the waist the new upper ribcage?

Whatev. The important thing is that my months of hard work are about to pay off. I'm ready to take on the fashion world for my second reporting assignment for *Scene*. Not that hiding in a limousine trunk on Oscar night was an actual *assignment*. Still, Nell Wickham – editor of the hottest celebrity magazine in the Northern Hemisphere – said she was proud and called me 'fearless'. She also called me Susie, Susan, Sue and Suzanne, but why quibble over names when I'm now known as the teen intern who can get the story no matter how much trunk lint it takes?

Sweet!

Today, as the leaves in New York City turn 'Golden Apricot' (one of the season's sizzling new colours,

FYI), I'm going to enter the epicentre of style: Fashion Week. The mere sound of those two words sends shivers of thrill up and down my spine. The world's designers will reveal their latest creations inside a monster tent in the middle of Manhattan. A tent that's for *insiders* only.

'Your press pass will get you in the front door,' said Sasha, *Scene* magazine's ga-ga Fashion Editor, 'and I can get you into a few fashion shows, but the rest is up to you. Nell and I will be busy. We can't babysit you.'

'I don't need a babysitter,' I say.

'Good. You only have one week, so make it count.'

Six-feet tall, mega-thin, latte-skinned, eyes halfway between sage and copper, Sasha makes *every* outfit count. She's beyond fashionable. If you want to know what will be in style tomorrow, look at what she's wearing today. Her indefinable accent sounds dipped in honey. Even though the fashion section of *Scene* usually features celebrity nip-slips caught by the magazine's seriously lush photographer, Keith Franklin, Sasha is a fashion diva. She oozes style. She was *born* hot. If they made designer diapers, she would have insisted her mother put them on her. Before I became a fashionista, I definitely would have fallen into the 'not' category. Unless you consider Gap jeans trendy. Which, silly me, I thought they were.

'Not the way *you* wear them,' Sasha told me, matter-of-factly, leaving me to wonder, How *else* do you wear jeans?

During fall's Fashion Week, I plan to find out. Inside the humungous white tent, everyone who is anyone will vie to see and be seen. (That's another fashionista word – vie. From the French *envier*. As in 'envy'.) According to Sasha, fashion shows will be running morning, noon and night on three separate catwalks (or runways, if you want to get technical). Celebs will be escorted to front-row seats, models will wow the crowd, fashion editors will make and break careers. Paparazzi! Stars! Supermodels! Oglers! Lindsay Lohan slipping in her Chanel boots!

How lucky can a 'not' girl get?

'Designer clothes are yet another way to enslave women in our male-dominated society,' Amelia, my bff, said at school today. 'Along with all sizes under ten, Botox, and Brazilian bikini waxes.'

'Does this long sweater make me look fat?' I replied.

Yep, I'm going *in*. My absolute fav place to be. Especially after my experiences in Hollywood. Nothing feels better than being on the *inside* of a velvet rope with a red carpet beneath your feet. Except maybe getting my first-ever article published in *Scene* magazine. Or riding in a limo with Randall Sanders. Or, okay, feeling my fingers curl around the muscular hand of a boyfriend who can't stop telling me how lucky he is that I finally agreed to go out with him after months of begging. I'm pretty sure that will feel *awesome*.

Here, back in reality, my heart rate is in triple digits. It's Friday afternoon and I'm in Bryant Park – the beautiful chunk of greenery behind the massive hunk of marble that is the New York Public Library on Forty-Second Street. You know, the library with the famous lions out front? Well, Bryant Park is their backyard. And twice a year, a gleaming white tent rises like a radioactive marshmallow on the Sixth Avenue end of the park. New Yorkers all know about the Fashion Week tent. But precious few are allowed in. Men in black guard the entrance. No one gets in without a pass. The tent encircles all that is fresh and hip and happening. Soon, it will encircle me, too – a bit *too* happening in the hip area, but fresh and flush with ideas.

My plan is simple: once I'm inside the tent, I'll blend in, scope out the scene, eavesdrop, interview models, and score a backstage scoop. Piece of (low-carb!) cake. How hard can it be to sneak backstage at a *tent*?

'Coming through,' I say, a bit wobbly on my new round-toed platform shoes. My press pass dangles proudly on my grey-sweatered chest.

As I weave through the crowd of tourists, I see television crews awaiting a celebrity sighting. They look hopefully at me, then quickly look away. Not that I care. The same thing happened on Oscar night and I got my own by-line in *Scene* magazine!

'Pardon *moi*,' I say, as I squeeze through the oglers and climb the stairs to the entrance.

Though I'm ashamed to admit it, I *do* cop a bit of an attitude. My eyebrow cocks as I pass the tourists in their elastic-waist jeans and fleece jackets. Channelling Nell, I look at them and think, 'How sad that I'm so of the moment and you're so not.' I even hear her British accent inside my head. A French phrase sneaks in, too. '*Quel dommage*'. What a pity.

'Susanna!' Sasha spots me climbing the front steps and dashes over.

'Sash!' I squeal, leaning in to air-kiss her cheeks. 'You look d-lish!'

'You dressed yourself?' she interrupts me, wild-eyed.

'*Oui*,' I reply proudly, striking a fabulous pose.

'I messengered clothes to your apartment. You didn't get them?' Sasha asks.

'Black trousers and black shirts,' I say.

'So?'

I stare at Sasha, agog. 'Grey is the new black and shorts are the new trousers!'

Sasha shuts her eyes and groans. Not the confidence-booster I was hoping for. Especially since I spent the past two weeks on a raw vegan diet.

'That trend is already tired to the point of dead. For you, Susanna, black will *always* be the new black. And shorts . . .' She glances down at the grey Bermuda shorts I bought at Bloomingdale's with my mother's employee discount and shudders.

At that moment, there's a commotion behind us on the steps. I don't have time to feel hurt. Sasha and I both wheel around. Me, still shaky in the high platform pumps I bought at Payless.

'Janet, Janet, Janet!'

The crowd chants and surges forward. Sasha grabs

my sleeve and yanks me through the entrance, into the tent.

'Nell is looking for you,' she says. 'Tomorrow, wear what I gave you.'

I nod, but I barely look at her. Janet Jackson just walked into the Fashion Week tent and she looks *magnifique*!

TW⦿

Not even one minute into my new assignment and already a superstar sighting! Wa*hoo*. Hobnobbing with the terminally chic is *so* much better than riding around in a trunk!

With bodyguards cushioning her, Janet Jackson is ushered straight past me. She wears black trousers and a black shirt, which Sasha doesn't fail to acknowledge with a cock of her own eyebrow in my direction. But, Ms Jackson looks nothing like I would look if I'd worn the clothes Sasha messengered to my apartment. The brim of her cap dips sexily over one eye; a long white jacket flows past her muscled thighs. Large hoops hang down from her ears. And there's that unmistakable smile. As she floats past me, I'm struck with the same thought I had in Hollywood on Oscar night: celebrities really *are* a different species. They're lit from within with stardust.

'It's mineral make-up,' Amelia said when I mentioned my 'stardust' theory. 'You, too, can look galactical.'

I rolled my eyes and sighed. Amelia is *so* earthbound. She's one of those effortless beauties – short, dark hair that falls perfectly; an athletic body that can handle a slice of pizza and two garlic knots without turning them into a muffin-top billowing over her jeans the very next day. Though Mel *was* interested in my adventures at the Oscars, I have yet to inspire true star worship in my best friend. She once said, 'Sam Worthington is too pretty to be hot.' How do you respond to something as absurd as *that*?

The Jackson entourage quickly moves out of sight, leaving me standing by myself inside the humungous white tent. Sasha is off being fabulous somewhere. Nell, for the moment, is out of sight. Though it's decidedly unfashionable, I allow my jaw to hang open while I take it all in.

Inside, it doesn't feel like a *tent* at all. Not that I'm at all familiar with tents. Camping among hungry wild animals and using leaves as toilet paper is *totally* not my thing. I'm more of a zoo girl. And scented quilted toilet tissue. But this tent, well, it's more like a magic white fortress than a collapsible building with canvas walls. Bright and sunny, the ceiling is sky-high and the room vibrates with the pulsing bass of distant loud music. Ba *bum*. Ba *bum*. It's huge ... and I'm only standing in the *lobby*. The actual fashion show catwalks are – you guessed it – behind velvet ropes at the far end of the *ginormous* room. Guarded by more men in black.

My first fashion show isn't for an hour, so I half-heartedly look for Nell while I stroll around the room and check out the scene. Yeah, I could call her cell to find out what she wants. But, why wake the sleeping beast? Knowing Nell, she probably wants me to rush out and find her a hat just like Janet Jackson's. No way am I going out when I just got in!

Making sure my press pass is facing outwards, I close my gaping mouth and subtly bob my head to the beat as I strut into the crowd. A tall girl in spiked heels and red tights hands me a free magazine. Another offers me a bottle of water. I guzzle it down, and grab another for later. Tons of Glitterati – beautiful people, according to my Fashionese lessons – are milling around, all pretending that they don't care what anyone thinks of them, but dying to be praised.

'Alandra, I'm loving those earrings.'

'Gar, your vest is *so* now.'

'Did you see what Jasmina was wearing? It screamed 1980s.'

Flashes of conversations fly by my ears.

'Zac Posen's show is the must-see.'

'Narciso is fabuloso!'

Smack in the centre of the tent lobby, there's a large stone fountain surrounded by mannequins in designer robes. Above it, like a humungous lampshade, a white gauzy sphere encircles several twinkling crystal chandeliers. At eye-level, flat-screen TVs face out, showing earlier runway shows. All along the edge are sponsor booths – Delta Airlines, Moet Chandon champagne, and the official Fashion Week hydrator: Aquafina. Free bottles of water are *everywhere*.

Note to self: bring bigger bag tomorrow.

'Excuse me,' a man with dyed-orange hair, a suit made of shower curtain fabric, and a matching puffy hat taps my shoulder. 'Where's the restroom?'

'I have no idea,' I say. 'Sorry.'

With a pained expression, he quickly prances away.

Second note to self: forget guzzling Aquafina until you find the loo.

Honestly, it's hard trying to look cool when I'm in

the middle of such a spectacle. I want to squeal and clap my hands like a kid at the circus. No one in my school could believe I scored such an awesome gig. It's September, school just started, and I'm already racing off after World History class to pad my future resumé. Ever since Nell Wickham brought me on board last summer to be her 'average teen' intern, my life has been anything *but* average. And a press pass to Fashion Week, well, it doesn't get better than that. (Unless a bonafide boyfriend was here with me. Maybe even a college boy, though my parents would freak.)

I do spot a smattering of Jersey girls with big hair and burgundy nail polish and arrogantly wonder, 'How did *they* get in here with *us*?'

'Excuse me,' I say, walking up to a Fashionista such as myself. She wears a white puffy mini-dress that looks like baby-doll pajamas. 'Can you point me in the direction of the *toilettes*?' I ask.

She's sucking on an Aquafina bottle, so I'm pretty sure she knows.

'It's ove—' Suddenly she stops. Her eyes scan my body from head to toe. '*Scene* magazine?' she asks, her gaze resting on my press pass.

'Yes,' I say proudly. 'I'm Susanna Barr—'

'Sasha let you out in that get-up?'

I blink.

'Did you rob a homeless man?' she asks, sneering.

Before I have a chance to mention that shorts are the new trousers, and grey is the new black, she says, 'Oh, I get it. You're a "*don't*". This is some special *Scene* magazine promotion, right?'

Crushed, I'm tempted to tell her that her whole look is tired to the point of being dead, but I'm dangerously close to feeling humiliation to the point of being drenched in sloppy tears.

Composing myself, I take a deep breath and say, 'I never got to finish telling you my name. I'm Susanna Barringer. You may have read my by-line in the Oscar-week edition of *Scene*? I was the "Girl in the Trunk". I'm the girl who gets the story everybody wants to read. No matter what. Which is exactly what I'm going to do here at Fashion Week. As soon as I find the bathroom. Now, before I was so rudely interrupted, I was wondering, do you happen to know where the restroom is located?'

Miss Baby Doll now blinks. My heart is pounding so hard it hurts. My cheeks are burning red.

'Over there,' she says, pointing. 'By that exit.'

'Thank you.'

Turning on my Payless heels, I make a beeline for the bathroom before the dam breaks in my chest and tears ruin the Silver Peony eyeshadow I spent twenty minutes applying this morning, and another twenty minutes touching up on the subway.

Fashion is not for wimps. I heard that once on a fashion TV show. Or did I read it in a magazine? Both, probably. It's a brutal business full of starving people who obsess over hair highlights and spend obscene amounts of money on a few pieces of fabric. While that may be true, I know one other true thing: I'm no wimp.

'Susan!'

My heart hits my stomach. I'd know that voice anywhere. Nell Wickham is the only Brit whose accent *doesn't* sound lyrical. In fact, right now it sounds hysterical.

'Where have you *been*?' she shrieks, yanking me out of the bathroom line.

'I have to use the toilet – what happened to your mouth?'

'You noticed, then?' Her hand flies up to cover her

puffy mouth. She looks like a character from *Finding Nemo*.

'Noticed what?' I say, too quickly, trying not to stare at the water balloons that were once her upper and lower lips.

'I told my dermatologist to make me look like Angelina Jolie, and he went collagen crazy. Angelina doesn't look like this!'

I'd have to agree. Though I decide against noting that Angelina was *born* with her lips. *Entertainment Tonight* has broadcast the kiddie photos to prove it. I also decide against asking Nell, 'What on Earth did you expect?' Instead, I deal with more pressing issues.

'I have to go to the bathroom.'

Nell glares. 'How could you possibly think of peeing when I need you?'

'Need me?' I ask. Can those two rafts be deflated somehow?

'Yes,' Nell says through gritted teeth. 'Get my lawyer on the phone. I want to sue.'

I look at her, confused. 'Didn't you just tell me that you *asked* him to pump you up?'

She raises one eyebrow. 'Do I look like Angelina Jolie to you?'

'No,' I say, 'but I do see a hint of Halle Berry and a touch of Nicole Kidman.'

I didn't spend an entire summer kissing Nell Wickham's insecure butt without learning a thing or two.

'You do?' she asks.

'Yes,' I say, matter-of-factly. 'I do.'

Nell's lips float skyward in a clownish grin. She pulls a hand mirror out of her bag and gazes into it.

'Yes. I see what you're saying,' she says.

It's all I can do to keep from groaning. The woman is totally mental.

She sighs. 'Though I did ask for Angelina, I guess Halle's okay.'

'Plus a touch of Nicole,' I add.

Nell's smile is the stuff of nightmares. But I don't let on. For now, she's feeling good about herself which means she'll go easy on me. I'll be free to score my scoop. If I could just get to the bathroom.

'I *really* have to go,' I say.

But Nell is no longer listening. Not that she ever really does. She's now obsessing over a freckle that the laser missed.

*

By now, the bathroom line is even longer. So I don't wait in it. Instead, I shake off Miss Baby Doll's slam and Nell's fish lips by marching straight out the tent's side door. I can always get back inside with my pass. And, there's still lots of time before my first runway show begins. Plenty of time to boost my confidence by using my sixteen years of training as a New Yorker to bluff my way into a bathroom.

THREE

For a major metropolis with one and a half million people, Manhattan is shamefully lacking public places to pee. Restaurant bathrooms are for patrons only, store toilets are only open to employees, hotel lobby restrooms require a pass key, museum facilities are beyond the entrance where you have to pay to get in, and the public library loo – just behind the tent in Bryant Park – is always packed. I might as well wait in the 'Aquafina' line inside the tent.

Not me. Not the Girl in the Trunk.

It's a sunny, beautiful day outside. The kind of fall afternoon that makes everyone love New York. Our air is electrified. Somehow, it even *smells* exciting. The cool fresh air makes us all feel like it's true: making it here really does mean you can make it anywhere.

Still smarting from being called a 'don't' by a girl who's so skinny she probably stopped having periods,

I spot my toilet target across the street. It's a large apartment building, with a doorman.

'You're a wily New Yorker, Susanna,' I say out loud, smoothing my long grey sweater over my shorts, careful not to twist my ankle on the uneven park pavement.

The doorman is standing beneath a green awning, gazing absent-mindedly at the spectacle in Bryant Park. Without being seen, I stash my press pass in my bra, and cross the street a few doors down from his building. Then, mussing up my hair, I slowly make my approach.

'I'm . . . uh . . . excuse me, it's just . . .' I say.

'Are you okay?' the doorman asks, gently touching my back.

'I . . . I . . . I'm going to faint,' I say.

Quickly, he rushes me inside the lobby and sits me down on a cushioned bench. Grabbing an LL Bean catalogue left by one of the tenants, he fans my face.

'Put your head between your knees,' he suggests.

I obey. After a few deep inhalations, I lift my head and smile gently. 'I'm feeling better now. It's my period, I think.'

He looks away. Fans more vigorously.

'I'm sorry to bother you,' I say.

'You're no bother, dear. Sit here for as long as you like.'

I sit, sigh, squeeze his kind hand.

'Do you, by any chance,' I ask, 'have a restroom?'

'Of course.'

Bingo.

All doormen in nice big buildings have their own little bathroom. It's one of those secrets New Yorkers know. And most doormen are *men*. Mention anything menstrual to a guy and he'll trip over himself not to hear about it again. Monthly periods are one of those mysteries of womanhood that guys find too bizarre to fathom. At least that's what my dad once told me. And he's a *scientist*. So, though I hate to use my gender for something dishonest, I do feel a deep sense of satisfaction that I have the required amount of subcutaneous fat to actually *have* a period. Unlike Miss Baby Doll *Be-atch*.

'Thank you *so* much,' I say, Oprah-like, letting him lead me into his secret bathroom.

It's not the cleanest toilet I've ever seen. Which can be expected since, according to my mom, 'Men are toilet-blind.' They can't see when a bathroom needs a good scrubbing. Or the garbage needs taking out, or the clothes need folding, or the babies need a diaper change (Mom has a whole list). Still, I'm grateful.

Emerging from the restroom refreshed and relieved, I smile and announce, 'I'm *so* much better now.' Which is the God's honest truth.

'Do you need me to call someone?' he asks. 'Your parents?'

'No, thank you, sir. I'll be fine.'

As I walk back out into the sunlight, I turn and wave at the helpful doorman. He grins broadly, knowing he did a good deed. Helped a damsel in distress. Honestly, I do hate to fib – especially to such a nice person – but it's known as 'City Survival'. He never would have let me in if I'd just asked politely. Creativity and female biology are always required. Besides, how could my wee white lie be wrong when I made someone feel so good about himself?

I feel pretty good, too. Who cares that I was just called a 'don't'? That snotty girl probably doesn't have a boyfriend, either. Who wants a girlfriend who dresses like a little girl?

As soon as I'm out of sight, I reposition my press

pass in front of my chest and confidently march back around to the front entrance of the tent.

'Aquafina?' the same water girl asks me.

'I'd love one,' I say.

My first-ever grown-up fashion show will be starting soon, and as every fashionista knows, it's important to hydrate.

FOUR

Mom took me to a fashion show once. It was a mother/daughter tea at Bloomingdale's. Though I was just a kid, I remember a lot of pink fur and sandwiches that were so tiny I ate about fifteen of them. I also remember how much I longed to look like the girls on the catwalk. Their hair bounced in perfect ringlets; their thighs didn't touch at the top.

'Seat assignments for the next show.'

My cheeks flush. My first Fashion Week show is about to begin. On one side of the lobby, a skinny girl with long brown hair and a walkie-talkie points to a line forming in front of a folding table. Like a school of fish, the fashionistas swerve to the table in unison.

Here we go, I say to myself. Excited, I pull my invitation out of my handbag and hold it proudly while I stand in line for twenty minutes. At least

I'm getting the hang of these platform pumps, I think. I don't wobble at all.

'Susanna Barringer,' I say, confidently, when it's finally my turn. '*Scene* magazine.'

Another skinny girl with long brown hair scans the list.

'Ah, yes,' she says, spotting my name to my utter relief. Then she picks up an index card and writes an 'S' on it.

'Thanks,' I say, taking my seat assignment and heading for the velvet rope with the other invitees. The 'In' girls, I call us, silently. Including the few boys that are with us. Are they fashion*istos*?

Glancing around, I scan the crowd for Sasha and Janet Jackson, but don't see them. They must be in a different show. I don't see Nell, either, which is fortunate. I'd hate to miss my very first Fashion Week show because my boss now felt peckish and had a hankering for chai tea.

Flashing my seat assignment card, I glide past the man guarding the velvet rope and silently squeal. My future is unfolding like a golden catwalk. My pulse races. I can't stop grinning. This is the most thrilling moment of my career so far. Though chatting with

Beyoncé after Randall Sanders' movie premiere *was* amazingly cool. But here, I'm in a world that's much more mysterious than monthly periods. I, Susanna Barringer, am about to enter the inner sanctum of *Fashion*.

First impression: it's *loud*. Jacked-up techno Musak, there's no discernible song, just a thumping beat that feels like CPR on my chest. The large room – which looks *nothing* like a tent – is totally dark, except for the bright white catwalk smack down the centre. Rows of seats rise up on either side. Photographers are clumped together at the end where the models will pose and turn around. Giant camera lenses sit atop spindly tripods. Keith isn't there because, as he told me, 'Fashion Week photo passes go to magazines that cover real fashion, not *celebrity* fashion.' When I asked what he meant, he showed me a photograph of Jessica Alba on a red carpet in a see-through green dress.

'Why would she wear that?' I asked, incredulous. 'With no bra?'

'Lots of stars don't realise how bright, and penetrating, a camera light can be,' he replied, adding, 'which is why I have a career.'

As I had in the tent lobby, I bob my head to the beat and adopt an attitude of *ennui*. Boredom. Been here, done this. I attempt to look like this is just another ho-hum day among the couture cognoscenti.

'Seat S,' I say to the usher, handing him my seating card.

My fingers are crossed. I know I'm not 'A' list enough for a front row seat – I doubt I even made the alphabet – but I am desperately hoping to be seated within earshot of *real* fashionistas like Gwyneth Paltrow, Mischa Barton or Evangeline Eastman, Nell's nemesis at *Spotlight* magazine.

'Standing room,' the usher replies. 'Up in the back.'

'Standing?' I swallow. 'There must be some mistake. I have an invitation.'

'An invitation just gets you in the show,' he says, his *ennui* completely real. 'Seat assignments are separate.'

'But—'

'Next.'

The Glitterati behind me push me into the room. They all have actual seats, apparently, and can't wait to sit in them. The pounding beat now feels like a hammer on my breast bone. *Standing* room? In platform pumps?

'Suck it up, Susanna,' I say out loud. Not that anyone can hear me. 'Fashion is not for wimps.'

Holding my head up, I climb the stands to the only row with no seats at all. The top.

'At least I'll be able to see over everyone's head,' I say, plastering a smile on my face. Then, I suffer another body blow.

'No!' I moan.

Each seat contains a gift bag. But there's zilch for the standers. How fair is that? No seat *and* no swag? I'm dying to see the fashion freebies. A Gucci bag? Manolo Blahnik shoes? Bobbi Brown make-up kit? Is it possible that Fashion Week gift bags are as awesome as they are on Oscar night? Even though they are now taxed, I'd happily pay Uncle Sam for some serious fashion bling. Can you even tax a sixteen-year-old who's only income is babysitting?

My head swims as my heart aches. I gaze longingly down at the *true* 'In' girls seated in the room, swag bags tucked neatly under their well-toned legs. At that moment, a gaggle of Jersey girls joins me in the standing section. My comeuppance is complete.

'Great view!' I shout over the music to one of them, making the best of it. But she just looks perplexed and pops a bubble of gum in my face.

FIVE

While fashion may not be for wimps, it is apparently, for those who wait. The show doesn't start for another half an hour. I'm beginning to wonder if this is all a big joke. Some *Punk'd* segment where we find out that *we* are actually the show. Which isn't too far off. As I look across the catwalk to the other side of the room, I see a guy with ink-black hair, a black cape, and a red fedora hat angled over one eye. What's up with all these hats? Is a hat the new hair?

I also see tons of air-kisses and finger wiggle-waves. Even from this height, I can make out the standard fashion greeting: 'You look *fab*ulous!' Not to be judgmental, but if you tell *everyone* they look fabulous, does anyone believe you?

Suddenly, there's a commotion in the front row. Television camera lights flash on and all eyes shift to a woman being interviewed. Is it Gwyneth? Paris?

Evangeline? An Olsen or two? I crane my neck until I can see her. Then, I can't believe my eyes. It's Ginger from *Gilligan's Island*. Hardly the celebrity sighting I was hoping for. I only recognise her because I once watched a *Gilligan's Island* marathon on late-night TV and dreamt I was Ginger for days. Is she some fashion icon for the assisted living set? Are they asking her how she kept that sparkly gown looking so fresh after years on a deserted island?

Eventually, the Ginger interview ends, the seats fill up and my ankles start aching. The show was supposed to start at four-thirty, and it's after five. I'd give anything for a tiny crustless sandwich.

Then, it happens.

The lights fade and the music gets even louder. My ears actually hurt. It's all bass. Ba *BUM*! Ba *BUM*! But, it has the desired effect. My heart beats in time with the music and blood shoots through my veins. If the first model doesn't appear soon, I'm quite sure I'll explode.

The crowd stares, breathless, at the far end of the catwalk.

I see a bare leg standing behind the wings.

Then, ba *BUM*! Ba *BUM*! The show begins.

'Hey!' I squeal, clapping my hands like a kid. The first model of my first-ever adult fashion show is wearing grey shorts, a long grey sweater, and round-toed platform pumps.

I, Susanna Barringer, am a fashion diva!

There's really only one word for what I'm witnessing: spectacle. The catwalk is a dazzling white landing strip. The model looks straight ahead, appearing bored. Skinny doesn't even come *close* to describing how thin she is. She's *sub*-zero. Same with the next model who emerges from backstage the moment the first girl poses and cops an attitude at the end of the runway.

The word that keeps rolling over and over in my mind is *alien*. Models, I can't help but notice, don't look anything like regular people. Thighs that don't touch at the top? Ha! Nothing touches, except their knobby knees. From my vantage point up top, I see that their hip bones jut out further than their non-existent boobs. Their arms hang like two pieces of rope, swinging behind their backs as they strut down the catwalk. And that walk! What's up with that? They look like prancing horses, one hoof crossing in front of the other. It's like they are all stepping over dog poop. Who walks like that?

Honestly, I can't say that any of the models look very happy to be there. No one smiles. Especially not the guys, who look slightly miffed to be wearing such silly clothes.

The show lasts about twenty minutes. Long enough for me to see that there is *lots* of grey. Lots of shorts. I feel vindicated. My outfit is totally in style even though my body will never be.

'Bravo!' the crowd shouts at the end of the show as all the models horse-prance out on the catwalk with the male designer. I can't help but notice that his body isn't even *close* to a male model's. He'd look silly in his own clothes. What's up with that?

As Ginger and the rest of the couture cognoscenti shuffle out of the tent – with their swag bags (aargh!) – I stay put and scope out the scene. A few photographers with hand-held cameras flash their passes at the men guarding the end of the catwalk that leads backstage. Ironically, these fashion photographers are dressed in what can only be called, 'anti-style'. Baggy old jeans, T-shirts that look like they were picked up from their bedroom floors, khaki vests with sagging pockets. Keith Franklin is *so* much cuter. None of these guys even wears a bandana!

There are emergency exit doors at the top of the stands, guarded by young interns dressed in long green T-shirts with Fashion Week logos.

'Can I get out this way?' I ask the intern in front of the door near me.

'No,' she says. As I expected her to.

'What's behind that door?' I ask, trying to sound innocent.

'Stairs.'

'Where to?'

The intern, a freckly face girl about my age, pinches her eyebrows together. This wasn't part of her training – answering nosy questions.

I grin sheepishly and say, 'I'm hoping to be a Fashion Week intern myself next year. I mean, how cool is it to see all these shows?'

She smiles. 'It's awesome.'

'Do you work for a specific designer? Or do you float around?'

'I work this *room*,' she says, tossing her hair in a way I totally recognise. The way I tossed mine earlier when I felt all superior to the Jersey girls.

'Man!' I say, admiringly. 'You're so lucky.'

She flips her hair again.

'So, does this staircase lead backstage?' I ask, slipping it in so subtly, I nearly burst into applause at my own stellar performance.

'No. Just outside. The only backstage entrance from the inside is down there.' She points to the heavily guarded end of the catwalk. My spirits sag.

'Ah,' I say.

The room is nearly empty. It's time to go.

'Thanks,' I say to the intern, turning to go. Then I stop. 'Can I ask you a question?'

'Sure.'

'Of all the shows you've seen, whose clothes do you want to wear most?'

She laughs. 'No normal girl can actually *wear* these clothes!'

SIX

'Thirty-three thousand dollars,' Amelia says, glumly, on the sidewalk in Times Square.

It's Friday night. We meet at our all-time fav spot in the city: the Virgin Megastore on Broadway at Forty-Sixth. Though I'm reluctant to walk under a humungous neon sign that reads, 'Virgin', I'm feeling good about myself. I survived Day One of Fashion Week.

'Frankly,' I say, sucking in my cheeks and striking a fabulous pose, 'I feel like a million bucks.'

Mel chuckles. 'I'm talking about Cornell's tuition. Yale is almost forty-six thousand if you count room and board.'

Gripping my best friend by the shoulders, I turn her around and say, 'Look up.'

She looks up.

Times Square is vibrating with a gazillion coloured

lights. Huge television screens air the latest news, giant ticker tapes run stock prices around the perimeter of buildings, gorgeous models smile down from humungous billboards, theatres flash names of the stars appearing inside. The black sky is on fire with neon. MTV's *Total Request Live* is across the street, Hershey's chocolate paradise is on the next corner, a toy store with a Ferris Wheel *inside* it is a few doors down.

'We're in the middle of Fantasyland,' I say. 'It's Friday night. For a few hours, can't we pretend that college is free?'

Mel shrugs. 'Might as well pretend we both got into Harvard, too.'

'There you go!' I chirp, kissing my best friend on the cheek. Arm in arm, we push the revolving door and enter Virgin's megaworld of music, books, movies and videos.

Seriously, I could live in this place. On the ground floor, there are listening stations to hear all the latest CDs. One floor down is where my parents would hang out, so I skip that. But, on the lower level, there's an underground café, a bookstore and movie theatres. What else does a person need?

'Wanna share a Rice Krispies treat?' I ask Mel. I've had a mad craving for sugar ever since I entered the Bryant Park tent. Hmmmm. Sigmund Freud is probably rolling his eyes in his grave.

'Yeah, cool,' Mel says.

Of course, I end up eating most of it. Mel is one of those people who could leave a piece of cake sitting on a plate and actually forget about it. I'm the type that hears it calling my name.

Susannnnna! Yoo hoo! Hellooooo! I'm down here!

As we sip cappuccinos and bob our heads to the loud beat of My Chemical Romance's song, 'Black Parade', I tell Mel about my afternoon. Even the doorman bathroom part.

'You didn't!' she says.

'I did.'

She tells me how she spent two hours helping a blind woman in her apartment building 'read' her mail.

'You didn't!' I say, but I know she did. That's the kind of girl Amelia is. Which is why I don't rag on her too much for not caring about celebrities. She cares about people she actually *knows*.

Just as I'm licking the foam off my cappuccino lid, Mel grips my forearm and squeezes.

41

'Don't turn around,' she whispers.

Of course, I turn around instantly.

'Susanna?'

The undigested Rice Krispies treat lands in my stomach with a *thud*.

'Ben?'

Awkwardly, I stand up and give Ben an even more awkward hug.

'You're so tall,' he says, bashing my cheek with his chin.

I want to explain about my rounded-toe platform pumps, and the fact that grey is the new black and shorts are the new trousers, but I'm speechless. I'm also blushing 'Hollyhock', another hot colour of the season. Ben McDermott is here, in the *Virgin* Megastore? Is this a sign from the gods?

'What are you doing in New York?' Amelia asks Ben, saving me.

'My parents split,' he says. 'Mom moved back into the city and I moved back with her.'

Ben McDermott lives in New York City again? Every synapse in my brain is shooting sparks. My heart pumps in my ears. He's still tall and skinny. His thick cinnamon-coloured hair looks like it's standing up even when he combs it down, and his red cheeks on his pale skin glow like he's just skied down the Alps. And those lips . . . I start to wobble on my platform pumps.

'Wanna sit down?' Mel asks. 'Hang with us?'

'Yeah. Cool.'

Ben sits down. Somehow, I manoeuvre my body into a seat next to him. Please God, I think, don't let me have a Rice Krispie stuck to my face, or a cappuccino moustache. Not now. Not when the only boy I've ever loved is mere inches away.

SEVEN

Though I know it's impossible, my brain feels hoarse from screaming inside my head. Ben, the boy I loved in ninth grade, is back in town? During Fashion Week? He shows up when I'm snarfing down carbs?!

'So, where are you living?' I ask him, tossing my hair casually.

'Upper West Side,' he says. 'You still downtown?'

OMG! He remembers where I live!

'Yeah,' I say. 'Same place.'

'Still at Lab High in Chelsea?' he asks.

He didn't forget our school, either!

'Yeah. You?'

'Saint Agnes.'

My heart flutters. I've seen those Saint Agnes boys in their white shirts and ties and dress trousers. *Très* British schoolboy. And, since it's a private school, they're all smart and college-bound. Unlike the guys at

45

Lab. Even though it's one of the best public high schools in the city, there are still *way* too many guys who think they'll make it in the NBA or become the next David Beckham.

'Cool,' I say.

'It's awright,' Ben replies, shrugging.

Just as my brain is starting to chill out and function properly again, Ben says, 'You look good, Susanna.'

He says the same thing to Mel, but smiles at me in that way he used to smile when he was all nervous. The smile that once pushed me over the edge. I'm *so* glad I'm wearing the latest runway style. Even if Sasha doesn't agree, and my legs are cold and my feet are killing me.

'You look good, too, Ben,' That's what I *try* to say, but my tongue suddenly feels too thick to get a full sentence out.

'Welcome home,' I say, instead. Then I just sit there, grinning. No way can I move or stand with this mad-thumping heart and these quivering knees.

Saturday morning arrives much too quickly. I'd give anything if it was still Friday night, and I was still staring into Ben's beautiful green eyes. Well, almost anything. I definitely wouldn't sacrifice my *Scene* magazine scoop. Not when it's Day Two at Fashion Week and I've barely made it through the tent's front door.

Today is my first full day on the job. I got up this morning, dressed in the clothes that Sasha sent me, and went to work. But, not before seriously reminding myself that I'm a professional reporter. I don't have time to think about the boy I fell in love with in ninth grade, came extremely close to kissing (thanks for bringing popcorn into my room, Mom, at exactly the wrong moment), and cried over for months when he moved to Chicago. Okay, maybe not *months*. But it was definitely more than forty-eight hours of major blubbery. Ben was the closest thing I'd had – and have ever had – to a bonafide boyfriend. And now he's back? In New York? My heart leaps up and down in my chest.

'Get a grip,' I say.

'Excuse me?'

A woman on the crowded uptown subway train glares at me. She's wearing a grey sweater, too! Though, her faded jeans are far from shorts. And those tired ballet flats do nothing to elongate her legs.

'Sorry,' I stammer. 'I was talking to myself.'

She sneers and grabs a pole. I glance away and force myself to stop thinking about Ben. Work comes first. I'll pull a Scarlett O'Hara and think about Ben tomorrow. Or Monday at school when I have time. Today, I won't clog my brain with the memory of his pale pink lips or the words he whispered in my ear just before Mom popped in and said, 'Popcorn?' Not when Nell Wickham is expecting me to blow the cover off the fashion world.

Yes, I'll think about Ben on Monday. During Web Design class while I'm waiting for my meta-docs to load.

This morning, the Bryant Park tent is *packed*. Loud music pounds my ears, the air swirls with the scent of a hundred expensive perfumes. I'm wearing the black trousers and black shirt that Sasha messengered over, and I must say, I look *fabulous*. She's right – black is definitely my colour. Even though Ben said I looked hot in grey. Well, he didn't actually use the word 'hot' but I hope he was thinking it. Not that I'm thinking about him. Not today. While I'm at work.

'Brownie?'

A hunky male model in a brown UPS uniform strolls by with a plate full of wrapped brownies. At least I *think* he's a model. Is it possible that a real UPS guy could be so cute?

'Would you like one?' he asks me.

Who can resist a free brownie?

'Thanks,' I say, blushing (of course). Who can control the surge of blood in your veins when a male model hands you chocolate?

As I unwrap the brownie while I stand in line, I notice I'm the only one who takes one. Not that I'm surprised. In this room full of toddler sizes, I doubt anyone would be caught dead eating a single M&M much less an entire brownie. But, I'm okay with that. Now that I've seen a model's bod in the flesh (and bones!), I'm working on embracing my curves. Who wants to look like a scrawny boy? *Boys* don't even want to look like a scrawny boy! I'm going to accept what nature gave me. An *appetite*. And, a pelvic structure that my mom insists will make it easy for me to bear children, though it makes it impossible for me to look *fab*ulous in tight jeans.

'Susie!'

Just as I bite into the brownie, and feel the soft cakey

chocolate spread over the roof of my mouth, my pulse quickens.

'Yoo hoo! Suzanne!'

It's Nell. Her voice is the sound of a rattle on a snake. When Nell Wickham calls my name – even the wrong name – terror shoots through my veins.

'What is *that*?' she asks, aghast, looking at my brownie in my hand like it's a dog poop.

Instantly, I feel like one of The Trips with his grubby fingers in the cookie jar. I try to swallow, but the brownie appears to be stuck to the roof of my mouth.

'A *blau*nie,' I say. 'I didn't have breakfast.'

Not entirely true since I bought a roll from the coffee cart at the subway stop. The word 'breakfast' exits my brownie-filled mouth sounding like 'bleckfeh'. Again, I try to swallow. What, on Earth, has happened to all my spit?

'Get rid of it,' Nell commands, still staring at the brownie like it's toxic waste.

With no trash can in sight, I wrap the remaining brownie in the napkin Mr UPS gave me and tuck it in my bag. Then I resume trying to swallow.

'Stand here, Suze.' Nell yanks me out of line and

places me at an odd angle close to her. Way too close. I step back.

'I said *here*,' she says, positioning me.

The brownie is becoming cement on the roof of my mouth. Where are the Aquafina girls when you need them?

'The lighting in this tent is atrocious,' Nell says, quietly. 'Use your head to keep me in shadow until they open the doors to the next show.'

'Your *yips wook* fine,' I lie through the chocolate.

'I know,' she says. 'But I ran out of Ambien last night and was tossing and turning for hours. My skin aged *years* overnight.'

Oh, brother.

The last thing I would imagine a boss would mean when she told me to 'use my head' was to block the harsh light of day from illuminating her wrinkles. But, this is Nell Wickham. So I stand tall and close and make sure her face is bathed in flattering tones of grey.

'Nell!'

Nell whips her head around, then whips it back. 'Damn! Here comes that cow, Evangeline. Don't move, Sue.'

'My *blau*ni—' I point to my throat.

51

'Evie!' Nell squeals, leaning in to air-kiss Evangeline, dragging me with her. 'You look *fab*ulous!'

'No more fab than you!' Evie replies, even less sincerely.

I recognise Evangeline Eastman right away. A younger version of Nell, she's the editor of *Scene*'s biggest competitor, *Spotlight*. If Nell hadn't hired me as an intern last summer – though the word 'hired' implies pay and interns don't even make subway (or roll!) fare – I definitely would have sent my clever letter to Evangeline. While Anna Wintour may be fashion's go-to editor, Nell and Evangeline are both celebrity divas. My skin tingles just being this close to Evangeline. She's *gorgeous*. Her shoulder-length blonde hair is shinier than Nell's, the skin around her blue eyes is not quite as creased. Like Nell, Evangeline looks like she spends most people's yearly salaries on her appearance. You just don't get skin that glowy without professional sandblasting. How could Nell think she's a cow? She must think I'm an entire herd.

I try to swallow again. The brownie is now a chocolate slug slowly crawling down my throat.

'Going to D&G?' Evangeline asks Nell.

'Absolutely.'

'CK? DK?'

'Wouldn't miss them.'

An Aquafina girl walks by and I reach for a bottle of water. But, before I can grab it, Nell yanks me back in place.

'I hear Y & Kei are this year's "it" couple,' Evie says.

'I prefer the classics,' Nell says. 'Perry, Calvin, Ralph.'

'How brave of you to stick with the older crowd where there are so many fresher faces.'

Ooh. It's getting interesting. I lean in closer. In fact, I'm so close, I feel Nell's temperature rise.

'Speaking of fresh faces,' she says to Evangeline, 'you could use a resurfacing.'

'Thank you,' Evangeline says, breezily. 'That means a lot coming from a woman who's had *so* much done.'

Nell smiles stiffly. 'I have a fabulous facialist.'

'Does she charge extra to cover those lips?'

I let out a laugh, then quickly turn it into a cough. I'm no longer interested in water. I'd rather choke on a UPS brownie than miss this! No amount of grey head shadow can conceal Nell's blazing cheeks. Evie's eyes are on fire, too. I swear, they look satanic. I don't even realise I'm grinning until Evangeline says, 'Do you mind?'

'Mind?' I say, ignoring the chocolate lump that's now lodged in my chest. 'No, of course not. Go right ahead.'

'This is a *private* conversation,' she says.

Suddenly I realise how ridiculous I look standing there, blocking the light, like Nell's conjoined twin.

'Susan is my assistant,' Nell says, adding, 'She's a personal friend of Randall Sanders.'

'You are?' Evangeline asks.

I am? Nell shoots me a look.

'Yes,' I say. 'Randy and I are, um, personal friends.'

Evie's face lights up. 'Are you the Girl in the Trunk?'

My face glows. 'Why, yes. Yes, I am.'

'I loved that article,' she says. '*Très* gutsy!'

'That's our Sue,' Nell says. 'Fearless.'

'Susanna Barringer,' I say, fearlessly, reaching out to shake Evangeline's hand. She grabs it, raises one eyebrow, and asks, 'Does Nell treat you well?'

She can't possibly think Nell didn't hear it since the three of us are standing there like bowling pins. Glancing quickly at Nell, I do a double-take: her eyes are wide with panic.

'Absolutely,' I say, careful to keep my head up high

enough to block the sun from betraying my boss's expression.

Still leaning conspiratorially toward me, Evangeline says, 'If that ever changes, call me. There's always a place for a fearless young reporter at *Spotlight*.'

The brownie wad hits my stomach with a *thud*. Did I just hear what I just heard?

'Gotta run,' Evangeline says, twirling on her spiked heels, leaving me standing tall in Nell Wickham's light.

EIGHT

Wow. Just when you think you know how life is going to unfold, Ben McDermott (sort of) re-enters your life, Evangeline Eastman (sort of) offers you a job and Nell Wickham (definitely) looks like she cares. Before I could assure Nell that I was loyal to *Scene*, she whirled around on her spiked heels (don't these women know that platforms are the new heels?) and left. Not, however, before she said, 'You could use a breath mint, Susan.'

I'm pretty sure Nell was just lashing out. The Frustration-Aggression Response, if I remember correctly from Psych class last year. What's better than brownie breath?

Oh well. I'll think about what just happened later, in Web Design class, after I think about Ben. Right now, Nell's gone, Sasha is missing in action, and I'm standing here with a major job to do: infiltrate backstage and find a story that blows the designer cover off the fashion world.

'Aquafina?' The water girl walks by and hands me a bottle.

The next fashion show is by a designer named Manuel. Last night, after my Ben encounter, I floated home and Googled the designer. Turns out, he's *two* Manuels – junior and senior. Both specialise in western wear. The senior Manuel is the man behind Johnny Cash's signature black suits and the Beatles' Sergeant Pepper uniforms. With his son, Manuel, their new line features everything from snakeskin jackets to blinged-out cow-boy shirts. I'm excited to see the show, and even more excited to bluff my way backstage afterwards.

'Next.'

As the check-in line slowly moves forward, I fish my invitation out of my bag. I know the drill. Even though I have an invitation, I have to wait in the seat assignment line to be told I'll be *standing* in the back.

'Malo is divine.'

A blonde woman with perfect red lips stands in line behind me. She talks to another blonde woman whose red lipstick is also perfect, though a slightly darker shade. They both look just like Nell and Evangeline.

'Herchcovitch is beyond fashion.'

'Ditto Heatherette.'

I can't help but stare, agog that these couture cognoscenti women look so much alike. Their highlights are identical, their buckle-laden handbags could be twins, both wear black cashmere shawls draped loosely around their necks, neither woman has a single expression wrinkle when she frowns.

'Luca Luca?'

'Love him, love him.'

They even sound alike. Glancing around the lobby, I see more clones. Older women are white-blonde, younger are golden blonde, and the very youngest are brunette. Most wear black, with splashes of colour here and there. The dresses are all similar, as are the shoes and handbags. Even their fingernails are polished and filed in the same squared-off, milky-pink way. That's when it hits me. Unless you're Sasha, or some weird guy in a cape or overgrown girl in a Baby Doll dress, fashion is really about *following*. You read fashion magazines, watch fashion TV and go to Fashion Week so other people can tell you how to look. And, how to *change* your look every six months! Is this liberation, or slavery?

'Name, please?'

Finally, I'm at the front of the line.

'Susanna Barringer. *Scene* magazine. Up*standing* citizen,' I say, letting her know I know my place.

'Row F, seat four,' she says.

'Seat?' I ask, my eyes wide.

She nods and takes my invitation so she can write the seat assignment on the back. Then she helps the fashionista behind me.

Acting casual, I stifle a 'whoopie' and head for the velvet rope that separates the outsiders from those who have been invited inside. The sitters like *moi*! And, as I find my seat, I try not to scream when I see the swag bag on my chair.

'Manuel is my favourite designer,' I squeal, though no one pays attention to me. I'm not, after all, in the *front* row. Still, as soon as I have enough money, I'm totally going cowgirl.

As it had been in the other show, the walls are black and the catwalk is lit bright white. Country music pounds in my ear. I hear a Willie Nelson song, don't recognise the rest. I can't stop smiling. I pick up my swag bag, feel its light weight. Trying to look casual, I sit down, smooth my black trousers, and place the bag on the floor. No one is tearing through their bag. Why look desperate? Instead, I re-focus on the job at hand and scope out the scene. There will be plenty of time later to see whether I got a trip to the Bahamas, a Rolex watch or a day at Bliss spa.

Sweet!

As I look around the room, I'm struck by another revelation: the inside of a Fashion Week show is just like a junior high cafeteria. The 'populars' are all in the front row, air-kissing one another, silently crowing over their swanky seats. They have the best table in the cafeteria – the one near the only window. It's filled with garden salads and the lemon wedges they use as dressing. If a nerd, or (gasp!) a fashion 'don't' has the nerve to sit next to one of them, they'll treat her like she has Ebola. Or worse, like she eats bread.

In the second row, there's a tangible air of longing. It's the junior high equivalent of the Drill Team, the Pep Squad, junior varsity footballers. They are close to being the chosen ones … yet so far away. Their cafeteria table is next to the 'populars'. They eat garden salads with blue cheese dressing and bacon bits.

On occasion, some have been known to secretly sprinkle on a few croutons.

Row Two is filled with women pretending to chat with one another. But it's all for show. They toss their heads back and laugh loud enough for the 'populars' to hear. Maybe a 'popular' will look their way and flash the smile they bleached last night? And, if the fashion gods are happy, a front-row diva will check out their outfit, their hair highlights, their Jimmy Choo shoes they saved months for, and nod with approval. *Quel* joy! From there, it's only a matter of time before they, too, will sit with the 'populars' and have the power to snub everyone else.

The next three rows up are filled with workers. I see reporters jotting down notes, men and women dressed in black trousers and shirts just like mine. The girls wear their hair in ponytails, the guys – what few are there – use their fingers instead of a comb. In school, they are comparable to yearbook staffers, or kids like Amelia who volunteer in the Palliative Care Unit at the hospital when most people don't even know what the word 'palliative' means (Mel told me . . . it means making dying people feel less pain). In the cafeteria, these are the kids who take their burgers and fries to any open seat.

The workers are on the job. This fashion show is only part of their day, not the event of their lives.

I'm sitting in the *fifth* row. The top row. I'm here with editorial assistants, reporters from newspapers that no one reads, and girls with faded home hair colour who somehow wangled an invitation to the show. Cafeteria-wise, I'm with the group who brown-bags it. Mathletes, band members, guys from the computer lab. And, though Sasha will probably go all mental, I'm wearing my Payless platform shoes having discovered that four-inch heels shave off at least five pounds.

Okay, maybe I'm not a fashionista after all. Still, I hold my head high. Cafeteria food sucks! I'm proud to be with the unfashionable brainiacs. Trends come and go, I tell myself, but intelligence lasts forever. Or at least until you're my grandparents' age and forget where you put the car keys *and* the car. True, it would be cool to have fab clothes and a hot body, but not if it means eating salads with lemon wedges, and knowing the dry-cleaner better than the bagel guy. I actually *like* being in the back row. When I have a seat, that is. From this height, I can see it all.

Nell and Sasha walk in and take their seats in the front row just as the lights dim. Evangeline Eastman enters and sits in the front row as well. The music swells. Applause breaks out, and the show begins. My heart pumps in time with the beat.

Okay, *this* I wasn't expecting.

The first model strutting out on the catwalk is a guy. Though it's hard to label anyone this beautiful as male. He's topless, and by the low rise in his tan leather trousers, I bet he's bottomless, too. The only thing covering his stunningly-perfect torso is a criss-cross of sparkly leather straps. A bandolier, if I remember correctly from some old western movie my parents rented the other night. You know, where banditos keep their extra bullets? Only *these* bullets are twinkling with light. Are they diamonds? Cubic zirconia? What-ever they are, *he's* gorgeous. His shoulder-length light brown hair is expertly tussled. His chin and upper lip are shadowed in stubble. I can't tell from way up here, but I bet his eyes are green. Like Ben's. But, more sea foam than emerald. Definitely something exotic. But, isn't this a *fashion* show, I think. Who could possibly keep their eyes on his outfit?

Several women emerge onto the runway next. I'm thrilled to see more shorts, but shocked to notice they are all braless. They have open leather jackets on, but nothing else. Not that any of the models have boobs. From what I've seen so far, the only models who wear bras – or need to – are from Victoria's Secret.

Manuel's line is a medley of blacks, greys, whites and tans. Lots of thin, flappy leather. Very urban cowboy. One female model struts down the catwalk in a white tuxedo jacket (no shirt!) and low-cut, super-skinny distressed jeans that reveal her perfectly flat stomach.

'Oh,' I say to myself, flashing on Sasha's earlier comment. '*That's* how you wear jeans.'

I like Manuel's stuff a lot, though I don't know where *anyone* could wear the sparkly bandolier. And I'd definitely wear a shirt (*and* bra) under those jackets.

Like the other fashion show I saw yesterday, this one is over in a matter of minutes. I feel like I did a few summers ago at Disney World. All that waiting for a ten-minute ride?

As before, the audience bursts into applause when all the models come out with both of the Manuels. I applaud wildly, too, but take advantage of the diversion to tear open my swag bag and check out my booty.

Shampoo?

I blink hard and look again. There's a small bottle of shampoo, and some conditioner. Like the kind you'd find in a hotel. There's also a little programme with the Manuels pictured on the back, and the fashions described in the middle. Yes, I notice, as I glance through it, that sparkly strap is called a bandolier. And this one is studded with *crystals*.

I also can't help but notice that Fashion Week swag bags – at least this one – are *way* worse than those at the Oscars. I definitely don't have to worry about paying taxes on a sample bottle of shampoo.

The moment the models exit the runway with the designers, the floor swarms with the 'populars'. Nell, Sasha and Evangeline are quickly swallowed up in the crowd. Slipping my shampoo bottle and the Manuel programme in my handbag, I take a deep breath, and say out loud, 'You're on, Susanna.'

Time to go to work.

Clomping down the bleacher stairs to the runway, I stop at the bottom to catch my breath. Then, I confidently march toward the men in black who are guarding the backstage entrance.

'Susanna Barringer,' I say, flashing my pass. '*Scene* magazine.'

My head up, I keep walking – straight into the guard's open palm.

'I need to see your *backstage* pass,' he says, blocking the door.

'Oh, of course,' I say, smiling. 'Silly me. It's right here in my bag.'

As I fish around in my handbag, photographers and reporters with real backstage passes walk around me.

'I just had it,' I say, 'I know it's here somewh—'

Suddenly, I stop. Pulling my empty hand out of my bag, I reach up to my forehead and stagger backwards.

'I'm . . . uh . . . excuse me, it's just . . .' I say.

'Are you okay?' the guard asks, alarmed.

'I . . . I . . . I'm going to faint.' My eyes flutter closed.

Instantly, he springs into action. Pressing a button on the earpiece he's wearing, he says, 'We have a fainter. I repeat, a collapse inside the Manuel show, at the end of the catwalk.'

'If I could just sit down,' I say, weakly. 'Backstage.'

'Help is on the way,' he says, leading me to a seat . . . in the *audience*.

Help? What's the matter with this man? All I want him to do is step aside and let me fake-faint so I can lie on the floor backstage and listen for my Fashion Week scoop. He doesn't budge.

'It's my *period*,' I say. 'Is there a restroom backstage?'

Patting my shoulder, he simply says, 'Hang in there, miss.'

'Maybe a glass of water? Any Aquafina back there?'

With stethoscopes dangling around their necks, two hunky paramedics appear out of nowhere and lift me out of my seat.

'I'm much better now,' I say, hanging on to their strong arms. 'You can put me down.'

One of them grunts a little.

'It's my platform pumps,' I say, lamely. 'They're super heavy.'

Together, the two men lay me on a stretcher, cover me with a blanket and roll me – I'm not kidding, *roll* me down the catwalk. Mortified, I try to cover my head with the blanket, but my arms appear to be strapped to my sides.

Dear Lord, I silently pray, *if you've ever loved me, please make sure Nell, Sasha and Evangeline have already left.*

'Where are you taking me?' I ask, swallowing hard. 'Honestly, I feel loads better.'

They don't answer. The remaining Glitterati stragglers stop air-kissing one another and stare, open-mouthed, as I roll past. I don't see Nell, Sasha or Evangeline (thank God), and the photographers are all gone (thank *GOD!!*). The last thing I need is the headline: Girl in Trunk Becomes Girl on Stretcher. At some point, I'm going to have to make my mark while standing upright!

'I can hop off now,' I tell the paramedic. 'Really, you can pull over anywhere.'

They roll me out a side door in the tent (whew! I don't have to roll through the lobby!). Outside, the cool air feels good on my hot face. I hear the tinkling music of the Bryant Park carousel, feel the bumpy park pavement beneath the stretcher's wheels.

'Honestly, it was just my period,' I squeak, trying not to panic. Are they taking me to the hospital? Are they going to call my parents? 'It happens every month.'

'Relax,' one paramedic says. Then, he opens the back door of an ambulance that's parked on the street. They slide me inside and climb in with me.

'The dizziness?' I say, 'it's all gone. Just my normal dizzy personality.' I add, 'Ha, ha,' but neither one of

69

them laughs. One slaps a blood pressure cuff around my upper arm, the other – the cuter one – shines a tiny flashlight in my eyes.

Does our medical insurance cover fake-faints? I wonder. Will my parents have to pay for this?

'How many fingers am I holding up?' the hottie asks.

'Three,' I say.

'Did you eat anything today?'

Do I have to mention the brownie? It was only a bite, after all. And I'm not going to eat them any more. After I finish the partial one wrapped in the napkin in my bag, that is. But after that, no more. I'm pretty sure Mother Nature didn't want me to embrace my curves quite so heavily. Can he smell the chocolate from inside my bag?

'I had breakfast,' I say.

He sits me up. 'Your colour looks good.'

'Thank you,' I reply. 'Black on black is definitely me.'

'Your *cheek* colour,' the less-cute, but still I'd-have-no-chance-in-hell paramedic says.

'Oh.'

'Do you think you can stand up?' he asks.

70

'Yes.'

With their help, I stand and climb out of the ambulance.

'All better,' I chirp, brushing the blanket lint off my black trousers.

'Drink this,' Mr Cutie says, handing me a juice box, 'and don't forget to have lunch.'

Forget a meal? I laugh to myself. Who does he think I am? Amelia?

'I won't,' I say. 'Thanks.'

Just like that, the drama is over. The paramedics nod and return to saving lives, releasing me back into the wilds of Fashion Week.

NINE

Okay, so that whole period-fainting thing isn't going to work every time. I can handle a mini defeat. I'm no wimp! I have the rest of the week to get my scoop.

Right now, I'm a little peckish.

It's another gorgeous fall day in the city. Like a bat, I doubt Nell will emerge from the dark runway rooms before dusk. Cool air kisses my face as I scope out the perimeter of the massive white tent. New Yorkers sit on benches sprinkled throughout Bryant Park. They sip cappuccinos, read the gargantuan weekend paper. Dogs lie asleep at their feet.

'A crap studio on the Upper East Side just sold for half a mil.'

'Have you had the calamari at Battali's new place yet?'

'The *vegetable* tasting menu at Per Se is over two hundred bucks.'

Real estate and restaurants. And sky-high prices.

The New York conversation. I hear people chatting as I walk.

'You can't even rent a decent apartment in Red Hook for less than thirty-five hundred a month.'

I step over the thick black cables that snake along the edge of the white tent. And I pass the thick-necked men who guard both backstage entrances. Rats! Clomping around the tent in my platform shoes, I'm disappointed to see that there aren't any gaps in the canvas. This tent is nothing like the scout-tent I slept under in my grandparents' backyard. This tent is waterproof, soundproof and *reporter*proof.

Not that I'm going to let a little canvas stop *moi*.

But, right now, that brownie in my bag is seriously calling my name. I find an empty bench and sit down.

'Beautiful day.' An elderly lady on the bench next to mine, smiles.

'Stellar,' I reply, sounding alarmingly like Nell.

The warmth of my bag has made the brownie even more gooey, even more luscious. Carefully, I peel back the cellophane wrapping. I want the chocolate sticking to my ribs, not the packaging. Taking tiny bites, I swirl the chocolate around my mouth with my tongue. I hit every tastebud – even the salty ones. I decide to eat like a model (not that a model would *ever* eat a brownie!) and stretch one small square of chocolate and flour into a whole meal. I wash it down with juice. As I take another tiny bite, I imagine I'm biting into a giant piece of cake, a slice of pizza, a meatball sandw—

'Hey!' I say, suddenly. 'That's *it*!'

'What is, dear?' the old lady on the next bench asks.

'Nothing,' I say, gobbling down the rest of my brownie (I have *got* to stop talking to myself!). The sugar in the brownie has shot straight to my brain and ignited a brilliant idea. It's lunchtime! Well, almost. Close enough. Why didn't I think of it sooner. *Food!* My all-time favourite pleasure. Second only to riding in a limo (back seat, not trunk!) with Randall Sanders or having a serious make-out session with my yet-to-be identified boyfriend who may end up being Ben McDermott. Who doesn't love food? Even models must love to eat though they do it so rarely. Who can resist free food?

I lick the last bit of chocolate off my fingers and leap to my feet. If I hurry, I'll have plenty of time to launch Plan B before the next fashion show begins.

Sweet!

*

75

Bryant Park has a limited number of eateries. The Bryant Park Grill – a beautiful restaurant with real food on real plates – is way beyond my budget. I pass right by it and circle around the tents to the north side of the park where four kiosks with the cutesy name "'Wichcraft" are attracting a crowd. One sells coffees, another sells ice cream, the third sells soups and salads, and the fourth – you guessed it – 'wiches. As in *sand*wiches. I see a guy standing next to the kiosk biting into a thick, delicious-looking sandwich on ciabatta bread. Crusty crumbs fall from his mouth like snowflakes. I get in line.

'What's that yummy smell?' I ask when it's my turn to order. Clearly, this is no average sandwich shop.

'Probably the Sicilian tuna with fennel, black olives and lemon juice on a baguette,' the girl inside the kiosk says.

'Sold.'

How could I resist? I mean, How could *she* resist?

While I wait for the sandwich masterpiece to be made, I step aside and call Mel.

'I need your help,' I say the moment she answers.

'And I love you, too,' she replies.

'Ha, ha. Are you home?'

'Yes. And I'm depressed. Can you believe Columbia charges a "Student Life Fee" of three hundred dollars per term? What ivy league student has a life? And why should we have to pay for it?'

'Good,' I say. 'You're online.'

'Your empathy is overwhelming, Susanna.'

'What does it matter what college costs?' I ask. 'We're both going to graduate knee-deep in debt.'

'Like I said,' Mel says, 'I'm depressed.'

'Before you leap off the Brooklyn Bridge, will you please look up something online for me?'

Amelia groans. 'Don't tell me you're looking for the girl some designer went to the prom with.'

'Are you telling me that *wasn't* the highlight of your summer?' I say, laughing as I remember our train trip to New Jersey last summer to find Randall Sanders' first love.

'Actually, pathetically, it was,' my best friend says. We both laugh.

'This time, I need to find the name of a model in the next runway show at Bryant Park.'

'Which show?' Mel asks.

I dig out the Fashion Show schedule and tell her.

'Which model?'

77

'Any one,' I say. 'I just need a real name.'

'Do they have real names? Aren't they all exotic like Irina and Ghislaine?'

'Ghislaine? Where did you pull that out of?'

Mel laughs. 'My brain is overstuffed with useless knowledge. What am I worried about? I probably won't even get into Columbia.'

'I hear Yale is offering a Useless Knowledge major next year.'

'That's worth fifty thousand!'

We both laugh. We've been having some version of this conversation for months. Ever since the end of school last year when the guidance counsellor called Mel into her office to tell her she had the grades to get into an ivy. I received no such summons. But Mel, my incredibly generous bff, includes me in her 'ivy' plans. Though my future plans revolve more around *microphone* plants in a celebrity dressing room than anything green crawling up a ridiculously expensive university.

'I'll call you back in five,' Mel says.

'You're the best.'

The sandwich is ready. I hang up, pay, and take a deep, self-satisfied breath. I, Susanna Barringer, am about to show the world you don't need an ivy-league education to succeed. All you need is a delicious 'wich, a model's name, and a backdoor entrance where they've never seen you before.

TEN

With my press pass dangling around my neck, facing out, I stand tall and march straight for the incredible hulk guarding the second backstage door.

'Hello there!' I say, confidently.

'Can I help you?' he asks.

I flash my pass. 'Nell Wickham of *Scene* magazine sent me over with a delivery for Tanya,' I say.

Of course the model's name is Tanya (actually, it's Tanya *D,* but I'm not sure if that's to distinguish her from another Tanya, or if becoming a rapper is her fall-back job). Amelia was totally right. Catwalkers don't have normal names. Tanya's co-models are Bruna, Snejana, Daiane, to name a few. I bet Naomi – the supermodel with the super-hot, cell-flinging temper – pronounces her name exotically. *Ny*omi. I've never heard her say her name, but I just bet she does.

'Tanya is a model with the Anna Sui show,' I say to

the guard at the backstage door. Thanks to my best friend's thoroughness, I pronounce Anna's name correctly. It's 'Swee', not 'Soo-ey'. Before Amelia called me back, she did a quick online search for an audio download of the designer's name. If that isn't Harvard material, I don't know what is.

'I'll only be one minute,' I say to the guard. Then, I hold up my pass again and repeat Nell's name for emphasis. 'Wickham,' I say, '*Nell* Wickham.'

He looks me up and down. I swallow. This guard could be an extra on *The Sopranos*.

'My boss is a real nightmare,' I whisper, leaning into him. Doesn't every employee feel that way? I go for common ground. 'She'll chew my head off if I don't see Tanya.'

He sighs. I see him softening. I move in for the kill.

'Pretty please?' I say, trying to sound cute and petite. 'With sugar on top?'

I swear, I haven't said that since I was a chubby kid trying to manipulate my mom into giving me more ice cream. And frankly, it's humiliating to trot it out right now, at Fashion Week, where ice cream is probably considered radioactive. But, I focus on the larger picture. According to my Harvard-worthy researcher, Anna *Swee* is one of the hottest designers at Fashion Week. The backstage scoop at the Sui show will be even cooler than the limo trunk scoop at the Oscars.

'In and out. I promise,' I lie. Which isn't a full-on lie since I'm *undercover* and the very definition of the word is, well, lying. Besides, my fingers are crossed underneath the 'Wichcraft bag.

'Okay,' the guard says.

'Okay?' I repeat, thrilled.

'Nell Wickham, right?'

'Right.'

'*Scene* magazine?'

'You got it.'

The guard swivels around, opens the backstage door, and I follow him – walking straight into his meaty back. *Whomp.*

'Tanya!' he yells.

My eyes fling open. He's *calling* her?

'That's okay,' I say, quickly. 'I'll find her.'

Casually, I try to step around him, but his arm blocks the doorway like a locked turnstile.

'Tanya D to backstage door two,' he says into a microphone he suddenly produces from his lapel, Secret

Service style. I hear the request echo inside on a loud speaker.

Tanya-a-a D-d-d to backstage door-r-r two-o-o . . .

My heart hits the floor of my stomach with a thud.

'Really, sir,' I say, 'I don't mind getting her mysel—'

In what I can only describe as an alien visitation, a model suddenly appears.

'Yes?' she says.

My mouth drops open. The 'wich bag slips out of my hands. Up close, Tanya D is the most striking woman I've ever seen. Even her voice is gorgeous. She's ten feet tall (or seems like it) and has straight blonde hair down to her waist. Her skin is pale and perfect, her eyes are light blue. There isn't a freckle, a bump or a pore visible on her face. It's like her skin is made of wax. She wears a black top and patterned skirt. A necklace that looks like giant dice circles her flawless neck. Fully clothed, I'm quite sure she weighs less than one of my legs.

'Tuna sandwich?' I squeak.

Tanya stares at me, confused.

'Nell Wickham sent this kid over with a delivery,' the guard explains.

It's not until I reach my hands up that I realise the sandwich bag has fallen to the ground. Two fingers on my right hand are still crossed.

'Oops,' I say, scooping the sandwich up and dusting it off.

'Food?' Tanya asks.

Now *I* feel like an alien. Bringing food to a model? And *carbs*? What was I thinking? I know what I was thinking – that the guard would simply step aside and let me in. Once backstage, I'd stash the sandwich to eat later, and blend into the pre-show chaos. I'd hide behind a clothes rack and listen to the models chat with one another. I'd find out how they *really* felt about the clothes they were wearing. Once they left for the runway, I'd continue to eavesdrop, uncovering how the make-up artist really felt about the model. I, Susanna Barringer, would blow the lid off Fashion Week by revealing the true cattiness behind the catwalk.

Clearly, I might as well have been thinking that there really *is* a tooth fairy and the cute paramedic and Ben McDermott will fight one another for the chance to be my boyfriend.

What was I thinking?

'Thank you,' Tanya says, graciously, taking the sandwich. 'How lovely.'

Then, she leans down and kisses both my cheeks. She even *smells* perfect. With a professionally-trained turn, Tanya pivots and disappears backstage.

My arms drop limply to my sides.

'Any chance Nell Wickham would deliver a sandwich to me?' the guard asks, chuckling.

I stare at him, blinking. Then, I ask, 'What would you like?'

'Seriously?'

'The grilled cheddar, ham and pear smelt awesome,' I say.

'Sold,' he says, grinning.

With a completely *un*trained turn, I rotate on my Payless platforms and head back to the sandwich shack. It's the least I can do. I did lie, uh, *undercover*, right to his face. Two sandwiches completely blows my budget, but I have learnt a valuable lesson: getting backstage at Fashion Week is impossible.

Well, impossible for anyone who isn't *moi*.

ELEVEN

It's Saturday night. A chilly fall evening. One of those nights where you zip up your leather boots and wrap yourself in a Shearling jacket (faux, of course) and cab it downtown. It's a night for clubbing, for being a single sixteen-year-old girl on the prowl. For meeting Ben McDermott in the Village and seeing if the spark is still ignitable.

I'm a New Yorker. I'm adventurous. Everything I could ever want is just outside my front door.

So, I'm sitting in my room doing homework.

'Ugh,' I say out loud. It's taken me *hours* to create the image maps I need for the fake site I'm building for class. I chose the Web Design elective over Aviation hoping there would be more boys in it. A decision I totally regret. Especially now that Ben is maybe, possibly, hopefully (?!) back in the picture. There are tons of guys in my Web class, but they wear plaid short-sleeved shirts tucked into chinos. With navy blue Keds. And, have they never heard of Proactiv, the cleansing system that cleared up Jessica Simpson's zits?

'Bill Gates was a nerd,' Mom said when I complained about the absence of hotties. 'Look at him now!'

I looked at *her*.

'He's still a nerd,' I said. 'If I'd taken Aviation instead, the boys might look like Leonardo DiCaprio.'

'He's a pilot?' Mom asked.

I just rolled my eyes. We'd sat together on the couch and watched him in *The Aviator* on DVD only last week. It must be true what Mom says: 'Having three babies at once uses up the last vestiges of your brain.'

'Come on, baby,' I say to my computer screen. I just inserted a meta tag for extra credit and it's refusing to work.

Since I currently have no boyfriend, nor faux Shearling coat, I agreed to stay home this Saturday night and babysit The Trips while my parents went out on a date. If you can call it that. Mom wanted to see some dumb Disney musical on Forty-Second Street. Like she said, all her brain vestiges are gone.

After a long evening of baby wrangling – our current

favourite game is me making mouth farts on their tummies – The Trips are now asleep, the apartment is quiet, and my meta tag just clicked in. Life is good.

Bzzzzzzzz.

The intercom buzzer startles me. I leap up and run to the front door before The Trips wake up.

Bzzzz—

'Yes?' I say, breathless.

Instantly, I recognise the voice over the intercom. I press the 'door' button and release the downstairs lock. I hear the elevator shudder as it rises. The doors open on the fifth floor with a loud *whump.*

'Nell Wickham sent me with a delivery.'

Amelia stands there holding a pint of Ben & Jerry's Half-Baked: chocolate and vanilla ice cream, mixed with fudge brownie bits and gobs of chocolate chip cookie dough. I melt right there on the spot.

'How did you know I was peckish?' I say, imitating Nell.

'Wild guess.'

Mel comes through the doorway and I hug her tightly. For the rest of the night, we eat ice cream, watch videos, and avoid obsessing over Ben McDermott by seriously discussing which character on the TV show

Lost we'd lose our virginity to. Amelia picks the actor who portrays Charlie Pace because she's a major *Lord of the Rings* fan. Me, I chose the hunky guy who plays Sawyer because, well, in a dim light, with your eyes squinting, he looks a teeny bit like Ben.

TWELVE

I wonder if the whole world would think our country is possessed by religious fervour if they could see Bryant Park today – *Sunday*. God's day. I bet money none of these fashionistas went to church before they pulled on their leggings, bubble skirts and to-die-for peek-a-boo halter tops.

Me, I'm wearing the same black trousers and shirt I wore yesterday. I know it's a fashion felony to wear the same outfit two days in a row, but as Sasha reminded me the morning of the Oscars, I'm *working*. I don't have to look hot (of course, I ended up walking the red carpet in linty work clothes, but who could have predicted that?).

Today is my last full day at Fashion Week. I have an invitation to one show in about an hour. Tomorrow, I'll be back in school, missing everything that happens here from eight in the morning to three in the afternoon.

Plus, subway time. So, I'm determined to get my scoop today. Not that I have a clue how to get backstage.

'A brilliant idea will come to you,' Mel said last night, after we polished off the last of the Ben & Jerry's. 'You just have to relax and let the Universe speak to you.'

I rolled my eyes. Mel's elective is Yoga.

Still, here I am outside in Bryant Park, staring at the impenetrable white tent, with no better idea. So, I sit. No, I'm not cross-legged in the dirt with my palms facing up on my knees. I'm on a bench, under a tree, summoning the Universe.

'Susanna here,' I mutter. 'Failed fashionista. All ideas welcome.'

I even breach every city rule and shut my eyes for a few minutes. Though, I hold my handbag in a death grip.

'The Grey Ant show was awesome!'

'Alice Ritter's colours are fab!'

'Badgley Mischka's silhouettes are to die for!'

The sounds of Fashion Weekers wash over me. I quickly open my eyes to see if a scoop may be walking by, but no such luck. Just more couture clones dishing about the shows.

'Okay, Universe,' I mumble, getting back to

business. 'Do your thing. I don't have all day.'

Actually, I *do* have all day, but don't want to spend it sitting here, clueless.

After about ten minutes, with the Universe totally giving me the silent treatment, doubt begins to bubble in my veins. What if I *can't* get a scoop? What if the best story I can uncover is that Alice Ritter's colours are fab? Who *is* Alice Ritter anyway?

I swallow hard. There *has* to be some way to get backstage. Think, Susanna! Again, I shut my eyes and grip my bag. Then, I take a deep breath and review my options: my press pass will get me into the tent, but not the shows. I have one fashion show invitation left. The lobby is fun for eavesdropping and people-watching, but not scoop-worthy. Fashion interns block the doors inside the shows, not that they lead anywhere. Guards check for backstage passes inside. Outside, the exterior entrances are harder to crash than Randall Sanders' location sho—

Suddenly, I gasp.

'That's it!' I squeal out loud, once again. But no one notices. Not that I care. I'm too excited. The Universe didn't give me this idea, Keith Franklin did! Why didn't I think of it before?

Leaping up, I grab my handbag and run down the park steps towards the subway. If I hurry – and Nell isn't peckish, fish-lipped or too brightly-lit – I can get home, get what I need, and get back in time to snag the fashion scoop of the century!

THIRTEEN

Dad once told me that the real difference between humans and animals is mankind's ability to grow from past experiences. Animals can learn, but do they *grow*? Of course, my father has had to revise his theory each time our government makes a bonehead move, or one of The Trips gets another Cheerio stuck up his nose. But I, Susanna Barringer, am determined to show Dad, Mom, and the whole world that I am a supreme human being who can use my past experiences to grow into a fabulous fashion reporter. A girl who can get the story no matter *what*.

I'm ready.

I have all the stuff I need in my backpack – not the most fashion-forward accessory, but hey, I'm working. I'll look stylish another time, like when Ben McDermott curls my fingers around his muscular hand and begs me to be his girlfriend. Or, when he whispers that same thing he once whispered to me just before Mom ruined my whole life by walking in the room.

'Focus, Susanna,' I say.

Since the subway took *forever* to arrive – in both directions – I get back to Bryant Park after my fashion show has already started. They let me in anyway, but make me stand in the back.

'Joke's on you,' I smugly say to myself. 'As soon as the show is over, I'll be standing back*stage*.'

In the midst of the eardrum-busting music and the skeletal braless models sashaying down the catwalk in fussy, frilly, definitely dry-cleanable clothes no normal women could (or would?) wear, I finalise my plans. My heart is pounding. Or is it the loud bass hammering my breastbone? Hard to tell. The only thing I know for sure, is that this is my last chance to get my scoop. After today, I won't be able to get to Bryant Park until school lets out. And I'm flat out of invitations. Unless something amazing happens in the tent lobby after about four o'clock, I'm majorly out of luck.

It's now or never.

I lay my palm flat on my chest and feel the thumping. Yeah, it's my heart.

The last two models down the runway nearly trip

over their overly fussy gowns. One has a long, thin sequinned train in back that gets tangled in her feet; the other looks like a wedding cake that may topple over any moment. I can't imagine either woman being able to sit down. They can't walk, they can't sit, and they certainly would never eat anything drippy in those dresses. Who would buy such a dress? And, at the cost of a semester at Harvard?

All of a sudden, the show is over. Cameras click wildly as the designer walks out on the runway with her models. She has jet-black hair and wears an all-white outfit. Her models tower over her. She blows a kiss to someone in the front row. Everyone is clapping. I don't recognise the designer, and I forget her name. So much for my fashionista lessons! Not that it matters. I have more important things on my mind – like sneaking backstage and hearing what the models really have to say about her . . . whatever her name is.

Camera-phones are in the air all the way up the stands. The music is still deafening. My thudding chest is starting to hurt. In the next moment, however, the catwalk clears and the crowd stands and surges for the exit. That's when I make my move.

'Excuse me,' I say, pushing through the mob as I

worm my way forward to a spot beneath the stands. There, in the darkness, I quickly open my pack and pull out my equipment: a clipboard with some paper on it and a headphone with a wrap-around mouthpiece (it's my dad's ... I have no idea what he uses it for, but it's probably to record some gross forensic info). Tucking the headphone wire into my front pocket, and holding the clipboard close to my pounding chest, I stash my backpack far under the stands. Then, I take a deep breath and dive in.

'I'm on it,' I say into the dead microphone that's wrapped around my mouth. Moving fast, I march directly towards the guards that are blocking the back-stage entrance. On the way, I grab one of the fashion interns.

'They need you backstage,' I say to her. 'Follow me.'

Then, I cup one hand over the earpiece as if I'm listening to more instructions. 'Right away.'

Walk like you belong here.

People believe what they think they see.

Keith Franklin's words are on a loop inside my head. Last summer, on the Randall Sanders' set, he taught me well. I acted like a total nutjob but no one questioned him at all.

'We're on our way,' I say into the mic that's connected to nothing. Startled, but silent, the intern marches with me. My whole upper body is pulsing. My cheeks are on fire. Still, inspired by Keith, I barrel down the runway. The two guards look like Rottweilers.

'Okay, okay,' I say, impatiently into the dead microphone.

Clutching the intern's green sleeve with one hand, and my clipboard with the other, I practically drag her to the backstage door.

'We're almost there,' I say, loud enough for the guards to hear. 'I'm bringing her myself.'

Catching his eye, I nod at one of the guards and point to the intern. At the same time, I say into the mic, 'We're at the door. I'll be there in ten seconds.'

Incredibly, the guard nods back at me and steps aside. Holding my breath, I flash a thumbs-up and rush the intern past him, practically pushing her backstage.

'What's going on?' she asks, alarmed.

Feeling the blood shoot through my veins, I don't answer. I'm waiting for the heavy grip of the guard's giant paw on my shoulder. But, I don't feel anything other than my heart going berserk.

'Did I do something wrong?' the scared intern asks.

I look at her, then I glance behind us. Nobody even blinks in my direction. The intern and I are beyond the impenetrable line of defence. We're backstage at Fashion Week and no one seems to care.

'No,' I say, grinning. 'You were perfect.'

Open-mouthed, she blinks at me. In one last flourish, I reach my hand to the earpiece and say into the microphone, 'What's that? You don't need the intern any more?'

Then, because I heard it on some TV show, I add, 'Copy that,' even though I have no idea what it means.

'Designers,' I say to the intern, rolling my eyes as I let her go. 'They're all bonkers.'

The befuddled intern leaves, but I stay.

I can't believe where I am.

I, Susanna Barringer, celebrity reporter extraordinaire, black-trousers-wearer, soon to be Ben's girlfriend (fingers crossed), former fashionista, rising star, am *in*.

What I see takes my breath away.

FOURTEEN

Cigarette smoke billows into the air.

'No smoking!' someone shouts. Another person yells, 'No eating, either, until the winter collections!'

Laughter flutters around the room. The scene is utter chaos. Couture gowns are being lifted past heavily made-up models' faces. Garment bags are zipped. Blow-dryers packed up. One model eats a strawberry while a stylist unties her laced-up boots. Another stands in her mini-bra and thong screeching, 'Where are my shoes? Who stole my shoes?'

No one answers.

'Those shoes were hideous,' a make-up artist near me mumbles. 'But not nearly as awful as the dress she had to wear.'

'Hey!'

Someone shouts as the thong-clad model throws a tantrum and starts flinging shoes in the air.

'Stilettos are lethal weapons!' someone else shrieks.

I quickly step out of the line of fire and survey the room. Every surface is covered with stuff – Q-tips, hairspray, cell phones, iPods. Everyone seems to be in a rush to get out.

'Excellent show!' The designer appears and struts through the centre of the room, clapping her hands over her head. '*Merci, merci.*'

The models and stylists applaud back. Even the angry model smiles sweetly and claps her hands. As the designer air-kisses the people who put on her show, I quietly crouch behind a full rack of long white linen jackets. I doubt anyone will notice me in this mayhem, but why take the chance? Hiding is much safer. I couldn't bear to get booted out after I so cleverly made it in. Besides, I'm hoping to catch a glimpse of a male model in his birthday suit. Yes, it's a bit pervy to peer out from behind a clothes rack, but it's not like I'm peeping into his bedroom window. Or is it?

'Your clothes are luscious,' says the make-up artist who just called them 'awful' behind her back.

The word, 'fabulous' is tossed up and volleyed around the room. How many people are lying, I won-der? There are tons of different accents, though I can't tell if they're coming from the models or the stylists. What's obvious is that everyone is eager to kiss the designer's butt before they clear out to make room for the next show.

From my hiding place, I see models shoving stuff into their handbags, make-up artists snapping their cases shut, dressers zipping up garment bags, hair stylists wrapping cords around their blow-dryers. I don't see anyone who looks like Mr Bandolier – dressed or undressed. Bummer. I'd love to ask a male model what it feels like to be prettier than most girls.

'Darling, is this yours?' One of the hair guys holds up a Starbucks coffee cup. A painfully thin model grabs it and says, 'Yes. It's my lunch.'

The far wall of the tent is lined with small tables. Each table has a lighted mirror on it and a folding chair in front of it. Racks of clothes hug the opposite wall, each outfit tagged with a model's name. There are rows and rows of ga-ga expensive shoes – now all messed up. Plugs and cords are everywhere. Overhead, intense lights heat up the room.

At the far end of the room, the designer is being photographed and interviewed by reporters who are actually allowed back here.

'I've always been inspired by nature,' I hear her say.

'Tree bark,' one model near me mutters to another. 'That collar was so stiff it gave me a haircut.'

They giggle together as one whispers, 'Did you see Catrine out there? She totally wobbled the whole way.'

'I heard Zita nearly fell on her arse.'

'If only she would fall on her face. Then I *would* believe in Karma.'

Ooh, I think, *talk about a* cat*walk*!

The models giggle some more, and I peer out from behind my curtain of clothes in time to see them take photos of each other with their phones.

'Hurry up, people! The next show is ready to come in.' The guard I bought the sandwich for marches through the room. I hear the cackle of his walkie-talkie as I slide back behind the clothes rack.

My knees are beginning to ache. Crouching in four-inch platform pumps has turned into a very bad idea. Still, I'm willing to suffer to get more dirt. If I can hide here long enough, this show will be out and a new show will be in. Then, I'll be able to see firsthand what goes into creating a 'flawless' fashion show.

Sweet!

I shift slightly to ease the burning in my knees.

Thank God I haven't been hitting the Aquafina too hard. I'd hate to blow my cover looking for the loo.

Suddenly, my ears perk up. I hear a reporter say to the designer, 'Manuel's muse is Marlon Brando. Who's yours?'

That's definitely a reporter-type question. Not that I'd ever ask anything so lame. What's a muse, anyway? And wasn't Marlon Brando size Extra Large? Isn't that a little hypocritical since Manuel's clothes were all on Extra Small models? With no boobs and probably no underwear, either. That's what I'd ask. If I had the chance.

Before I can hear the designer's answer, I feel the tickle of soft linen against my face. Then I feel a gust of air. In a *whoosh*, I'm suddenly out in the open. Crouching behind *nothing*. Someone rolled my rack of long linen jackets away! I feel as naked as a model in a thong.

'What the—?' The rack-roller shrieks the moment he spots me. 'Who are you?'

Beet-faced, I try to stand up, but my knees appear to be locked. Plus, there's nothing to hold on to. No one, I notice, steps forward to give me a hand. Admittedly, I must look incredibly odd squatting there behind nothing. Like some African hunter out on the savannah.

'I, uh, er, well . . .' Form a sentence, Susanna! I shriek in my head. But nothing coherent comes out. Thinking fast on my *haunches* has never been my strong point. Too late, I realise I should have prepared a ready explanation in case I got caught.

'*There's* my earring!'

'This *isn't* the bathroom?'

'I've crouched and I can't get up.'

Something like that. But, as it is, I'm tongue-tied, lock-kneed, and utterly mortified. I'm now also being stared at by every person left in the room. Especially the designer.

'Who *are* you?' she asks, leaving the reporters to stand menacingly over me.

'Susanna Barringer,' I squeak.

'What are you doing here? Someone call security!'

Uh-oh.

'I'm—' In an attempt to get up gracefully, I fall down on my butt, and roll over onto my knees, doggy-style. Once again, I'm incredibly grateful to be wearing trousers. Though my previously fashionable grey shorts would have worked perf—

'*What* are you doing here?' The designer bellows at me in the tone of voice I've heard from my dad – the kind that says, 'I'm not going to ask you a third time.'

A reporter from the end of the room has taken notice. I see him salivate as he rushes over. At that same moment, the security guard races in and recognises me. My heart sinks. Is one sandwich enough to entice him not to blow my cover?

'Uh, I'm—'

'She's with me.'

All heads turn to the sound of a female voice. A voice I recognise.

'Get off the floor, Susanna,' she says. 'We have work to do.'

I struggle to my feet, stunned. The designer walks over to the woman who saved my arse, kisses her cheek and says, 'Evangeline, darling. You look *fab*ulous. What did you think of my show?'

FIFTEEN

Susanna? Evangeline Eastman just met me yesterday and she remembers my name? Nell has known me more than a year – she's even cried in front of me – and I'm still Sue, Susan, Susie, Suzanne, or (ugh!) Suze? Once, she even called me Anna!

'Grab a few strawberries for me, will you please?' Evangeline says to me. 'I'm famished.'

I scurry over to the giant fruit platter at the back of the room and pile several strawberries on a plate. Since she's being so nice, I throw in a couple of pineapple slices, too. The security guard saunters over.

'You're working for Evangeline Eastman now?' he quietly asks me. 'What happened to Nell Wickham?'

'I'm, um, a freelancer,' I say. 'Pineapple?'

The guard narrows his eyes at me. 'Don't make me regret not throwing you out.'

'I won't. I promise.'

With that, he returns to his post at the back door and I breathe normally again. By the time I return to Evangeline, the room is nearly cleared.

'Thank you, Susanna,' she says when I hand her the fruit plate.

Please? Thank you? My head is spinning.

'Have you ever been backstage at a Fashion Week show before?' she asks.

I almost burst out laughing, tempted to confess that my only backstage experience was our middle school's production of *Grease*. My job, as assistant stage manager, was mostly to make sure no one forgot their lines. Which everyone did. The guy playing Doody even barfed before he went on.

'No,' I say, trying to sound blasé. 'I'm a Fashion Week virgin.'

Evangeline chuckles. Though it was a totally dumb thing to say. I stifle the urge to throw my arms around her and tell her how much I love her. Instead, I blurt out, 'Nell will kill me if she sees me with you.'

'Why is that?' she asks.

'You're, well, the competition.'

Rising one eyebrow, she says, 'Hardly.'

Now I chuckle, though I feel really guilty about it.

Evangeline asks, 'Do you want me to tell security that you're *not* with me?'

I swallow. 'No.'

'I didn't think so. Between you and me, Susanna, Nell's days are numbered. God, she's over fifty.'

I flash on Nell's obsession with microdermabrasion and the latest injectables. Now I see why she wishes the world were candlelit.

'Nell is the past,' Evangeline says. '*You* are the future.'

'Me?' Beaming, I lower my head and blush.

'Unless you have somewhere else you'd rather be, Susanna, I suggest you stay right here and brace yourself. The real show is about to begin.'

If I'd had more time to process what just happened, I might have handled things differently. I might, for example, have said, 'Nell and I are both the future.' Or something loyal (and self-serving) like that. But, I don't have time. I'm swept up in the moment. Backstage before a fashion show is like walking into a tornado. Even if you hold on, you're going to be blown away.

In an instant, the room fills with people again.

They're different, yet they all look the same. Hair stylists wear black. Several guys have spiky tattoos encircling their buff upper arms. Everything that was packed a few moments before is unpacked now. Music blares. Blow-dryers blast. The air thickens with hairspray. As each skinny model comes through the door, she's whisked over to a table where a team of stylists await. I'm reminded of *The Wizard of Oz*. The whole scene is like Dorothy's makeover before she ends her trek down the yellow brick road. At one point, I count eight people on one model – two working her hair, two painting her face, one on each arm massaging in bronzing gel, and one on each foot for a pedi. The model, who looks about my age, winces each time a stylist yanks her hair.

Evangeline saunters around the room, chatting with everyone. Clearly, she has no fear of bright white light. I saunter, too. Or, the best imitation I can manage in my clunky platform shoes.

'The look is tamed lioness,' I hear a make-up artist say. 'Wild in a sex kitten sort of way.'

He paints the model's eyelids a glimmering gold. The hair stylist teases her hair so high it looks like a tumbleweed.

'Ouch,' she squeals.

'Sorry, love,' the stylist says. But he keeps teasing.

As soon as the model's hair and make-up are done, she's led over to the clothes rack. One dresser helps her take her street clothes off, while another helps her put her designer clothes on. I can't help but notice there's a vast difference between the two wardrobes. Almost every model arrives in jeans and a T-shirt. If they weren't walking skeletons, and ten feet tall, they'd look like everybody else. I'm shocked to notice that most aren't even very pretty. Professional hair and make-up artists really work magic. I wonder if I'd even recognise Tanya D if I saw her first thing in the morning.

'Catch her!' someone shouts near one of the clothes racks. There's a slight commotion, but no one stops working. Peering through the crowd, I see a model being lowered to the ground. Her long designer gown billows out all around her.

My God! She fainted. For *real.*

'There's an ambulance out front,' I shout, pushing through the crowd. 'I'll get a paramedic!'

The dresser rolls his eyes. 'Paramedic? If you want to help, pick that dress off the floor. It's ten-thousand-dollar couture.'

Like a high school marching band in perfect formation, the dresser protects the gown while a stylist grabs a juice box from the food table and her assistant picks up the shoes that have fallen off the model's feet. No one seems overly concerned. They certainly don't call the paramedics the way the guards did when I fake-fainted. In fact, they seem more annoyed than concerned.

'Cigarette crash.' Evangeline appears behind me and whispers in my ear. 'The first of many.'

Confused, I just blink.

'Models are always fainting before a show,' she explains. 'When you substitute smoking for eating, your body rebels.'

'Drink up, sweetie,' the stylist says, poking the apple juice straw into the model's slack mouth. 'Don't worry. It's fat-free.'

Backstage, it's complete chaos until the final nano-second before the model jettisons out on the catwalk. Someone is frantically adjusting, fluffing, lifting, or smoothing every inch of the model's look before she horse-prances before the audience, looking bored.

'This is really an acting job,' I say to myself. 'And

models are meant to be walking mannequins. No wonder real women can't wear these clothes!'

Just like the other fashion shows, this one is over in an instant. It reminds me of Thanksgiving dinner. You shop and bake and stuff and roast for hours. Still, no matter how hard you work on preparing the perfect meal, it's always over in twenty minutes or less.

The fainting model manages to walk up and down the catwalk in three different outfits. After the show, I ask her, 'Can I get you a sandwich or something?'

Pale and wobbly, she lights a cigarette and shakes her head, no. 'I have another show tonight.'

As I'm preparing to ask her a more probing question, like, 'Is your vision of heaven a Krispy Kreme factory?' my eye catches a terrifying sight. Nell is back-stage, kiss-kissing the designer.

'Excuse me,' I blurt out. Then I dive behind the nearest rack of size zeros.

'Your evening wear is fabulous!' I hear Nell say to the designer. 'I must have that fuchsia gown!'

'Fuchsia?' Evangeline's voice rises above the buzzing in the room. 'Aren't you a bit *mature* for hot pink, Nell?'

Peering out from between the gazillion dollar couture gowns, I see Nell's cheeks go hot pink.

'Evangeline, darling,' she says, 'You look so healthy. So plump.'

'Not as plump as your lips,' Evangeline replies.

Nell chuckles and shoots back, 'At least my lips aren't the only part of my body that's thin. Poor dear.'

The designer makes an excuse and a fast exit as I look at Evangeline and wonder, 'What is Nell talking about?' She's gorgeous, has a great body and normal lips that don't look like they're filled with helium.

'It must be hard maintaining your weight through menopause,' Evangeline says, smiling serenely at my boss.

'I wouldn't know,' Nell replies.

'Oh, of course not,' says Evangeline. 'Silly me. Anorexics don't have periods, do they?'

My jaw drops to the floor. I've never heard anyone speak to Nell this way. Oddly, I feel sorry for her. Even though she tortured me last summer and continues to treat me like her personal slave, I hate to see my boss get her comeuppance right in front of me. It's like seeing someone caught in a lie. Yeah, it's justice. But it's still squirmy to witness.

'If that were the case, Evie, you'd have *two* periods a month.'

Ouch.

Nell turns her back on Evangeline Eastman and reaches into her handbag. In the next moment, my cover is blown.

Look at this photograph. Every time I do it makes me laugh . . .

The Nickelback ringtone I downloaded into my cell plays loudly as I scramble to answer my phone. But, by the time I get to it, Nell has exposed my hiding place and is standing over me, glaring.

'Oh, hi,' I say, clambering to my feet. 'You look fabulous.'

'I just called you. What are you doing here, Susan?' Nell demands. Not the first time I've been asked that question while crouching behind a clothes rack.

'I'm, uh—'

'She's with me.'

Evangeline suddenly appears. Nell now glares at her.

'What are you talking about? Sue is my intern.'

'Her name is Susanna, Nell.'

'Sue, Susanna, Susan – what's the difference? She's still my intern.'

'Is she?'

Evangeline smiles angelically at me. Nell goes pale. I swallow hard.

'What do you say, Susanna?' Evangeline asks. 'Don't you think you and I would make a great team?'

I blink. Try to swallow again, but my mouth is suddenly the Sahara Desert. Nell looks indignant. Evangeline looks expectant. Both are waiting for to say something, but my brain has gone numb.

'I . . . I . . .' I splutter. With no better idea, I slap my hand over my forehead and say, 'I feel faint.'

Then, I slowly crumple to the floor in a heap. Nell groans. Evangeline helps me into a chair, and a stylist grabs a juice box from the fruit table and hands it to me.

'Thank you,' I mumble. After taking a sip, I look at my current boss and possible future boss and say, 'I need some air.'

With that, I get up and clomp my Payless platform shoes right out the door.

SIXTEEN

'Keith?'

It's Sunday afternoon. Keith Franklin is probably lounging in bed with a Fashion Week model who has the day off. Maybe he's feeding her a piece of lettuce, or giving her a sip of apple juice so she doesn't faint on him. Or under him. What*ev*. I need to talk to someone I trust. So, I chance it that his cell is on, and hope he's not *too* occupied to take my call.

'Susanna?' Keith says right away. 'Are you okay?'

'Yeah,' I say. 'Well, no. Not exactly. Physically, I'm fine. Emotionally, I'm – can you meet me?'

'What's going on?'

'Or I could meet you. I need to talk to you today, if possible. I mean, if you're not too, you know, occupied.'

Keith Franklin sighs. Even when he sounds exasperated, his sigh still revs my pulse. I picture him in a loft downtown. His black curly hair is mussed; one shiny

119

ringlet falls past his forehead. The *New York Times* is spread all over his dining room table. He drinks black coffee. There's a ring on the *Book Review* section where he places his mug. I don't see a model in the picture. Perhaps she's passed out in the bathroom.

'Meet me at Balthazar for a drink,' he says, finally.

'A drink?'

Keith sighs again. 'Does everyone forget you're a kid, or is it just me?'

I laugh. 'I'm hardly a kid, Keith. I'm sixteen.'

Now Keith laughs. 'Okay, Susanna. I'll be at Balthazar in an hour. Meet me there for a Coke.'

Of course Keith Franklin would hang out in a restaurant bar like Balthazar. It's a cool downtown bistro with white mosaic tiles on the floor, red leather booths and sky-high ceilings. The moment you step through the glossy black doors, it feels like you're in Paris. Not that I've actually been to Paris, but it feels like the Paris I've seen on television. And I'm *not* talking Paris Hilton.

'Susanna!'

Keith calls to me from one end of a humungously long bar. He's sipping something clear in a small glass with ice. Seeing him again makes me grin absurdly. After working with him last summer at *Scene* and last winter at the Academy Awards, I'm no longer a babbling idiot in his presence. Those amazing blue eyes don't make my knees feel all mushy any more. But I can't say I've regained full control of my central nervous system yet.

Keith stands and kisses my cheek. Okay, my knees *do* feel like pudding, but I recover quickly by sitting on one of the barstools.

'It's good to see you,' he says.

'You, too.'

After all we've been through together, neither doubts that it's true.

'Diet Coke, please,' I say to the bartender, trying not to look like I'm Keith's geeky little sister. Which, of course, I totally do.

'So . . . here I am,' Keith says. 'What's so urgent?'

I take a deep breath. 'It's Evangeline.'

'Evangeline Eastman? From *Spotlight*?'

'Yes.' My Diet Coke arrives and I take a sip.

'Go on,' Keith says.

'I think she offered me a job.'

*

Okay, if I were totally delusional, I'd say Keith Franklin and I were on an actual date. After about ten minutes at the bar, he suggests we have brunch.

'Brunch?' I repeat. 'It's almost three o'clock.'

'So what?' he says. 'I'm starved. I haven't eaten all day.'

Come to think of it, I'm a bit starved, too. Crouching behind clothes racks can work up an appetite.

'Okay,' I say, my central nervous system sending a blush to my cheeks. Even though my *brain* knows it's not a date, the capillaries in my face are acting like it is.

We leave the bar area and walk into the dining room. The maitre d' beams and warmly shakes Keith's hand. They act like old friends. He leads us to a booth in the back. *This*, I think, *is the most beautiful restaurant I've ever seen*. It doesn't hurt that I'm sitting next to one of the most beautiful guys I've ever seen. I bet Keith would look *awesome* in a crystal-studded bandolier.

'*Salade niçoise*,' I order, trying to sound mature, though I really want the brioche french toast. With bacon.

'I'll have the usual,' Keith says.

His 'usual' is a plate of fluffy scrambled eggs that smell like butter, and skinny french fries.

'Start at the beginning,' Keith says, scooping up a forkful of eggs, 'and tell me everything.'

Between bites, I do. Even Nell's fish lips and her attempt to use me as a beach umbrella in the tent lobby, though I leave out the brownie part. Don't guys prefer a little mystery? I also tell him how grateful I am that he taught me how to bluff my way backstage, though I admit I'm still stumped for a scoop.

'People already know that models are anorexic and hairdressers are catty and backstage is a circus,' I groan.

'Nell doesn't want you to rediscover the wheel, Susanna.'

'What does that mean?' I ask.

Keith says, 'You don't have to uncover something no one has ever heard of before. Your job is to report on the way *you* view Fashion Week. Susanna's take on the event. Your sixteen-year-old perspective will always be fresh.'

'Even if I think that fashion is a way to enslave women in a male-dominated society?' I ask, quoting Amelia.

'*Especially* if you think that,' he says, laughing.

As always, Keith Franklin makes me feel like I can do anything.

By the time the waiter clears our plates, I ask Keith what I came here to find out.

'Should I take a job at *Spotlight*? Would I be stabbing Nell in the back?'

Keith inhales loudly, then leans across the table and takes my hand. This time, my central nervous system only sends me a mild jolt.

'Nell and Evangeline have been rivals forever,' he says. 'No offence, Susanna, but Evangeline doesn't want you as much as she wants to stick it to Nell.'

'Oh,' I say.

'She must think you're valuable to Nell or she wouldn't care.'

'Oh?' I brighten.

'You want my advice?'

'Definitely.'

'Tell Evangeline that you're happy at *Scene*,' Keith says. 'Tell her you love working with Nell. And don't take the job – whatever she offers you. If you end up working for Evangeline Eastman, you'll be walking into a hornet's nest. And, trust me – you'll be the one who gets stung.'

I nod. After hearing it out loud, I know he's right.

The waiter brings the check and Keith hands him his credit card. Smiling, I think, *This is exactly what a date with Keith Franklin would feel like! How cool is this?*

'That reminds me,' I blurt out. 'I was hoping I could ask you for one more piece of advice.'

'Sure. Shoot.'

My heart starts tap dancing again, but I clamp my eyes shut and go for it.

'What's the best way to let a boy I used to know, know that I'd like to know him better? Know what I mean?'

Keith flings his head back and laughs.

I add, 'If any one of my three brothers wasn't still pooping in his trousers, I'd ask him. Besides my dad – who freaks out when I talk about boys – you're my only go-to guy.'

Grinning and looking *gorgeous*, Keith insists – again – that I tell him everything. Which I do. I even tell him what Ben McDermott whispered in my ear that night, in my room, before Mom ruined everything by popping in with popcorn.

Once more, Keith Franklin teaches me how to bluff my way in. *In.* My absolute fave place to be.

SEVENTEEN

Web Design class is a nightmare. My header tag refuses to repeat on every page, and the flash graphic I did for extra credit takes so long to download I'd be better off with an ordinary nav bar.

Not that I care.

I have a whole new plan today. Thanks to Keith, I now know how to get my scoop and (hopefully!) get Ben McDermott, too.

First things first.

I'm a professional reporter. I have less than a week to compile my unique take on Fashion Week, one that knocks Nell's socks off. There's no time to waste, so I get busy right there in Web class.

'I'd like to change my web design project,' I announce to the computer sciences teacher, Mr Vaynor, just before class begins.

'Oh?' he replies. 'In what way?'

'Every way. I don't want to build a website any more. Now, I want to start a blog.'

'You'll need an enticing subject,' he says.

'I have one. The Body Blog.'

'Good name,' he says.

'I want to create a space where girls can post their true feelings about fashion and size zeros and so-called style. Like, what's wrong with having a normal body and wearing last year's jeans? Why do we allow someone else to dictate how we should look? I'm not saying we should snarf down fast food and trans fats, but have you seen a model up close? She's *breakable*! Not to mention at risk for lung cancer. And fashion, well, it's *total* manipulation. Designers want me to get a new wardrobe every six months so they can get a new Ferrari every year! Or a beach house! Why should I, literally, buy into it? Why? Why? It's time to stop the madness.'

Mr Vaynor laughs. 'I see that you feel passionate about this, Susanna,' he says.

My neck feels warm. 'I do,' I say.

Suddenly, I realise the *true* impression Fashion Week left on me. I feel *angry*. Fashion isn't about style . . . it's about sales. And no wonder the models girls try to copy are impossibly skinny. What better way to fuel the gazillion-dollar diet industry!

'The time has come for all girls to take back their bodies,' I say.

Mr Vaynor smiles.

'I'd like to get extra credit, too,' I add brazenly.

'For what?'

'I'm going to publish my findings in *Scene* magazine.'

Mr Vaynor raises both brows. 'Has your boss at *Scene* already agreed to this?'

'No,' I say. 'But she will.'

He laughs. 'If you can pull it off, Susanna, you'll not only get extra credit, you'll ace this class.'

'Get ready to give me an A plus,' I say.

My teacher stands up and shakes my hand. Then he says three words that have become my new mantra: 'Go get 'em.'

Exactly what I plan to do.

I skip the next few days of Fashion Week to stay after school and work on The Body Blog. To avoid Evangeline and Nell, too, which, I've discovered, is the best way to deal with both of them. Well, the *easiest*, at least.

Creating a blog turns out to be much easier than dressing up a website. I want The Body Blog to look good, but mostly, I want it to inspire honesty. So, the first thing I do is have one of the nerds in Web class take a full-body photo of *moi*. Admittedly, I suck in my stomach and stand up extra straight. I secretly wish I was wearing my platform pumps, too, and the slimming black trousers Sasha gave me, but my normal height, size and old Gap jeans make a better point. Next, I download a photo of a model on the catwalk. It's not hard to find a super skinny one. They *all* are. I also include celebrity fashion shots – Ellen Pompeo from *Grey's Anatomy*, Victoria Beckham, the Olsen twins, Eva Longoria. Then, posting the famous images beneath my ordinary one, I pose the question, 'Have images of models or celebrities ever made you feel fat and ugly?'

The last thing I do is create a dialogue box and a submit button. To get things started, I post my impressions of Fashion Week.

'For all their high fashion expertise, I saw more followers than actual style-setters. Almost everyone appeared the same. And they *all* looked to the designers to tell them how to dress the same next season.'

Sasha will probably kill me when she reads this.

She's one of the few fashionistas who has a style all her own. But, as Keith Franklin told me, Nell wants *my* teenage take on Fashion Week. And this is how I feel.

'I couldn't help but wonder,' I also post in The Body Blog, 'are designers *afraid* to put real bodies on their runways because their clothes only look good on walking mannequins?'

If no other girls think the way I do, my plan will tank. My article for *Scene* will sound like the sour grapes of a chubbette. Admittedly, I probably wouldn't feel the way I do if I looked the way Tanya D does. But, that's the whole point. Hardly *anyone* looks like Tanya D! Why try to model ourselves after a model who looks so different from real girls she appears to be beamed up from another planet?

'Go get 'em, Susanna,' I say out loud.

And I do. By the last day of Fashion Week, my blog is on the net. I've attached it to all the contacts on my Hotmail list, asked them to attach it to all the contacts in their email, and asked them to ask *them* to attach it to their contacts. That ought to give me a good sampling, I think. Now, I sit back and pray for blogstorm.

And, oh yeah, I ask Ben McDermott out on a date.

EIGHTEEN

If I'd learnt how to *stop* the excess cutaneous blood flow that makes my neck and cheeks flush whenever I'm nervous, last year's Physiology class would have been totally worth the effort. As it is, however, I only learnt how to identify what's making my body freak out, not how to control it. Good thing Ben can't see me sitting in my room, on my computer, seriously pink, as I compose an email to him.

'I hope this is still your email address,' I begin. Then I delete it. What a stupid way to start! If he changed his email address, he'll never see it. If he still has the address he had two years ago, it won't matter.

I start again.

'Dear Ben,' I write. Then I stop. Am I my grandmother? *Dear?* How am I going to sign it, 'With fondest regards'? Am I one hundred years old?

I delete and start again.

'Hi Ben,' I type. 'How r u?'

Lifting my cold hands up to my hot cheeks, I examine the first sentence. It's a little lame, I conclude, but workable. After all, I can't just plunge into the one sentence Keith Franklin told me to say. The phrase that will, hopefully, inspire Ben to see if a spark is still there. Or can I? What if he has a girlfriend? Some hottie in Chicago. What if he cried when he had to leave her? Are they planning to get together at spring break? Will she fly out to New York? Of course she would! Who wouldn't want to come to New York? Or will Ben see her when he's there visiting his dad?

My mind races as my heart sinks. Of course Ben has a girlfriend! How could he not?

Then, I remember how he gazed at me in the Virgin Megastore when he said I looked good. You don't have that twinkle in your eyes when you have a girlfriend in Chicago. Or do you? Was he just playing me? Did he look at Mel that way, too, only I didn't notice? Are there none so blind as those who will not see?

'Susanna,' I shout. 'Enough!'

I know me. Insane inner dialogues can last for hours. If not days. And I have too much to do to waste my time in whackville. I inhale deeply. Why not take the

134

plunge and follow Keith's advice? Keith Franklin is, after all, a relationship expert. Who has more hands-on experience?

'Go get him, Susanna,' I say.

And I do.

'Hi Ben,' I write. 'It's *moi*. Wanna pick up where we left off?'

NINETEEN

The last day of Fashion Week is Friday. I don't have an invitation to a show, but I hang my press pass around my neck and head over to Bryant Park anyway. I'm wearing the clothes I wore to school – jeans, a Gap hoodie and my platform shoes. My hair is pulled back in a loose ponytail. Admittedly, my cutaneous blood flow is on overdrive, but I have one more job to do as a reporter: stroll around the lobby of the Fashion Week tent – dressed like a normal girl – and take note of the reaction (in the interest of full disclosure, I was planning to wear sneakers, but my platform pumps really do make me look slimmer and I'm not quite ready to fully embrace my curves in a lobby packed with fashionistas).

What a difference a week makes! My initial thrill at hearing the pounding music and seeing the Glitterati has totally faded. Maybe I'm just projecting (another term I learnt in Psych class), but everyone seems tired to the point of desperate. Like they can't wait for the spectacle to be over so they can kick off their shoes and eat a pizza in front of the TV. Like I said, I may be projecting.

'Coat check?' A face-lifted woman in black dashes up to me inside the Bryant Park tent.

'Excuse me?' I say.

'Where can I check my raincoat? I'm late for the next show.'

'I have no idea,' I say. 'Sorry.'

'You don't work here?' she asks, alarmed.

'No. I'm a reporter. For *Sce*—'

Before I can finish my sentence, she races off, her leather boots stomping across the hard floor. Agog, I reach in my bag and pull out my notebook.

'Barely five minutes in,' I write, 'I am mistaken for the help.'

Then I add, 'Clothes equal class? Is high fashion how the rich keep the poor "in their place"?'

Stashing my notebook, I continue my stroll. What I see stuns me, though it doesn't surprise me at all. The fashionistas either subtly sneer as I walk past or, most often, quickly look me up and down and, as quickly, turn away. No one smiles. No one steps aside if they're in my path. Mostly, I'm treated as if I don't exist. I'm so clearly not one of them, I'm invisible.

'Susanna?'

Wheeling around, I come face-to-face with Evangeline Eastman.

'Oh, hi,' I stutter, instantly mortified to have her see me dressed as I usually am. Just as I'm about to apologise for how I look, I stop myself. *Wait a minute!* I scream in my head. *What are you doing? Why should Evangeline make you feel bad about being who you are?*

'What's up?' I ask, my chin high (though, admittedly, I suck in my stomach).

'Where's Nell?' Evangeline says.

'I haven't seen her.'

Evangeline wears dark grey shorts over black tights, a light grey cashmere sweater that extends past her thighs, and round-toe platform pumps. She looks (sort of) like I did the first day. I nearly burst out laughing.

'I like your outfit,' I say.

'A Malo original,' she says. 'Straight off the runway.'

Evangeline then gives me the once-over and reaches her hand up to clutch my arm.

'My God, Susanna, has someone died?'

'Died?'

'You look so *awful*. What's happened?'

Now I do burst out laughing.

'Everything's fine,' I say. 'In fact, I'm ready to go home and work on my article.'

She leans close and asks, 'Have you thought about my offer of a job?'

'Yes, I have,' I say.

'And?'

'And I really, really appreciate it, but I'm happy where I am.'

'You are? With Nell?'

I lift my head and look around. I, Susanna Barringer, state school junior, ordinary girl, extraordinary reporter, am standing in the Bryant Park tent during Fashion Week. A few months ago, I was in Los Angeles at the Academy Awards. Before that, I walked the red carpet leading to Randall Sanders' movie premiere. I am the luckiest girl in the world.

'Yes,' I say, truly feeling it for the first time. 'I love working for Nell. I'll stay with her as long as she'll have me.'

Evangeline raises one eyebrow and scoffs. Then she turns and flits off to kiss-kiss the cheek of a woman who looks just like her.

TWENTY

Waiting. It's my least-favourite thing to do. Well, behind cutting out carbs, changing three stinking diapers at once and pretending to be a fashionista when I'm clearly not even close. Today is Saturday. Fashion Week is over. I'm sitting in my room in front of my computer staring at a blank blog. Amelia hasn't posted anything yet and she has *tons* to say on the topic. She told me she will, though, as soon as her mind isn't bogged down by the pressure to get into an ivy.

'Since Harvard ended its early admissions programme, everyone else probably will, too,' she moaned over the phone last night.

'What if nobody posts on The Body Blog?' I moaned back. 'What if Ben totally freaks out and never speaks to me again?'

So, I'm sitting here. Waiting. My blog is empty and Ben hasn't responded. I'd rather be changing three loaded diapers.

Ping!

All of a sudden, a blog comment pops up on my screen. My heart nearly leaps up my throat and onto the keyboard.

'Peacocks, lions, Silverback gorillas – in almost every species, the *male* animal is the pretty one. Why do humans insist on decorating women? Are we more gullible? Because we don't say no?'

'Yes!' I shriek, clapping my hands.

Ping! Another submission pops up.

'Designers *want* us to feel bad about our bods so we buy their clothes 2 feel good.'

Ping!

'Fashion is Capitalism, pure and simple. Designers create demand 2 fuel their supply.'

Ping! Ping!

'I've hated my body all my life. I'm not fat, I'm just not perfect.'

'OMG. I hate my nose. And my teeth.'

Ping!

'Me 2.'

Suddenly, like a band just started to play, The Body Blog becomes a raucous party. Words pop up and dance across my screen.

'The average catwalk model weighs 110lbs and is 5'9".'

'Not in Madrid. Yay Spain! They set a min wt at 121 lbs.'

'Still *very* thin if ur 5/9!'

'I'm 5 ft. 4 and I weigh 130 lbs. Aargh!'

'Susanna?'

In the midst of all the chatter, and my blaring CD player, I barely hear my mother call me from the living room.

'*Susanna!*'

'What?' I yell back. 'I'm busy.'

'Someone's here to see you.'

'Amelia?' I call out, watching another post pop up on the blog. 'Send her in!'

Ping!

'Have u heard about vanity sizing?' someone writes. 'Designers deliberately mark their clothes w/ wrong – smaller – sizes so we feel like we r thinner. It's all bull s***.'

Behind me, I hear my bedroom door open.

'Mel,' I call over my shoulder. 'My blog is going wild!'

'It's me.'

My hands freeze on the keyboard keys.

Whipping my head around, I'm stunned to be face-to-face with one of the most beautiful faces I've ever seen.

'Ben?!'

He grins and my whole body melts into my desk chair.

'What are you doing here?' I ask.

Ben looks down, bounces the tip of his sneaker against the leg of my desk and says, 'You said something about wanting to pick up where we left off?'

TWENTY-ONE

Just when you think you know how life is going to unfold, Ben McDermott appears in your bedroom. For the sake of my *Scene* magazine exposé on the shallowness of the fashion world, I wish my first thought wasn't, 'OMG! I'm wearing sweat-pants.' And, for the sake of my potential relationship with Ben, I wish the capillary loops in my face weren't engorged with blood making me look beet-red.

'Popcorn?' Mom pops her head through the door, making the scene all the more surreal.

'Yeah,' I sputter. 'You remember Ben, don't you, Mom?'

'Yes, of course. We got reacquainted in the living room.'

Ben was a few feet away in our living room while I was sitting here in my sweat-pants? I have got to stop listening to a CD while I'm online!

Mom leaves to throw a popcorn bag in the microwave, making sure my door is wide open. Ben asks, 'What are you working on?' peering over my shoulder at the exact moment a blog post appears saying, 'What's the big deal? Wear what you want to wear.'

I press the 'off' button on my monitor and inhale him. I remember that smell. Soap and hair gel.

'Nothing,' I say, spinning around in my chair. 'Just something I'm writing for *Scene* magazine.'

'*Scene* magazine?'

Ben's eyes pop out of his face. At that moment, I realise how much has changed since he moved away two years ago. I've walked the red carpet at the Oscars! I've met Randall Sanders' mom and been nose to nose with Beyoncé. I've felt the spray of the Pacific Ocean on my face.

'Have a seat, Ben,' I say.

He sits on the edge of my bed. My cheeks are burning and my pulse is racing. I can tell that he's nervous, too, which makes me nearly burst into tears. Don't ask me why. I guess my central nervous system has gone insane. Even though we emailed one another at first, our friendship dribbled off into nothingness. I never thought I'd see him again. Now, here he is.

Right where we left off.

That sentence he whispered in my ear two years ago is pinballing through my brain.

'Sanna!' My little brother, Evan, comes toddling through the door holding a cooled, puffed up bag of popcorn. Henry and Sam follow, with three more popcorn bags. They look so cute I can't help but drop to the floor and scoop all three into my arms. Instantly, we're a wriggling mass of diapers and giggles.

'Sack the quarterback!' Ben shouts, joining us on the floor. He grabs a bag of popcorn, curls up in a ball and yells, 'Fumble!'

'Fumble!' my brothers squeal. And, like three puppies trying to get at their dinner, they pile on Ben.

'Flag on the play,' he calls, laughing beneath the pile-up. 'Time out!'

But it's too late. The Trips are all over him. Their chubby little fingers reach for the popcorn bag, their stubby bare toes wedge their way into every nook on Ben's coiled body. Evan drools. Henry is red from laughing. And Sam is nearly upside down. It's hilarious.

'Help!' Ben calls out.

I laugh. 'You sacked the quarterback,' I say. 'You're on your own.'

'Sack the *cor*back!' Henry shouts.

By the time Ben gets out from under the attack of the Three Stooges, loose popcorn is everywhere. Sam's baby-fine hair is electrified and standing straight up. Evan has an unpopped kernel stuck to his damp cheek, Henry is shoving popcorn in his mouth, and Ben is flushed and grinning. I sit opposite the four of them and smile. It's a mess of drool and sagging diaper-pants, but it's the most touching moment I've ever seen. I'm certain my heart is going to burst open and flood the room with red.

Without thinking, I roll onto my hands and knees and crawl over to Ben. Popcorn crunches beneath my palms. Sam waddles over and tries to climb on my back. I don't care. All I can see are Ben's fiery green eyes, his rosy cheeks and the rise and fall of his chest as he rests against the side of my bed. Crawling right up to him, I gaze into those amazing eyes and whisper the three words he said to me, in this very room, two years ago.

'You are beautiful,' I murmur.

Then, I lean in and let my lips press against his. We

kiss. His lips are soft; mine are a little chapped. I'm in sweats, my hair is a mess, my make-up is gone with the wind, my baby brothers have now surrounded us. Nothing is the way I've imagined this moment to be. Yet everything is perfectly right.

TWENTY-TWO⊙

How can *anyone* work when they're in love? The Body Blog has gone bananas. I've got posts from all over the country. And outside the country, too! My computer *pinged* so many times during the night I had to turn it off. And now, Sunday morning, when I should be blogging back and starting to write my *Scene* magazine article, all I can do is obsessively check my phone for TMs.

'Want 2 hang out l8er?' Ben texted me earlier that morning.

'Y. WN?' I replied, trying to sound oh-so-casual.

'Whenev,' he wrote back, sounding way *too* casual.

'3?' I suggested, taking the bull by the horns.

'OK,' he replied, without texting anything more specific.

All I could do was ask, 'WHR?' Which I did. Now,

153

I'm obsessively checking my phone to read his response. So far, zippo.

'Susanna?'

Mom calls me from the living room. My heart lurches. Is Ben here again? Instinctively, I look down and check out my outfit. Jeans and a white T-shirt. Not too hideous, I think.

'Yeah,' I call back, sounding as sexy as I dare with my mom listening.

'I need to run to the store,' she yells. 'Can you watch the boys?'

Oh.

'Sure,' I say, standing. It'll be nice to have a little break. But, she better be home by two-thirty, I think, so I have time to get ready to hang with Ben by three. Assuming he texts me back telling me where we should meet. Or should I text him?

I grab my phone so I can obsessively check it while I watch my brothers.

'Mel? It's me.'

How, I wonder, can anyone fall in love without discussing every detail with their bff?

'That's a movie scene!' Amelia chirps over the

phone when I tell her about the popcorn kiss.

'Help me figure out how to make a sequel?' I plead.

Laughing, my best friend suggests potato crisps all over my bedroom floor, but I veto the idea because no way could I focus on Ben with yummy crisps all over.

While I talk to Mel, I wipe all the remnants of breakfast off my brothers' faces. Then I put them in their playpen so Amelia and I can plot out my next move without interruption.

'You're not going to like my advice,' she says to me.

'Uh-oh,' I reply. 'What?'

'Tell Ben you can't see him today.'

'*What?!*'

'You're a working girl, Susanna. Don't you have an article to write? Aren't you trying to blow the lid off the fashion world?'

'Yeah, but,' I stutter. 'Mel, it's *Ben.*'

My best friend takes a deep breath and blows it into the phone. 'Consider this,' Mel says matter-of-factly, 'if you let a boy derail your career after one kiss, what will happen when you go all the way?'

She has a point. Just *thinking* about losing my V to Ben makes it hard to concentrate on anything else. Fashion Week is over, I have loads of Blog submissions, and Nell is expecting my unique take on the entire extravaganza ASAP so she can publish it in the next issue. Not to mention my extra credit in Web class. I *do* have loads do.

'What if he won't wait for me?' I say, sounding insecure.

Mel's voice is firm. 'Any guy who won't wait for a girl to finish her work before play isn't a guy you want in your life.'

'I guess you're right,' I say, softly.

'Of course I'm right,' Mel says. 'Now, stand up and walk over to a mirror.'

I laugh.

'I'm serious,' she says. 'Tell me when you're staring at your face.'

Walking over to the bathroom mirror, I groan and say, 'I need a haircut.'

'Look at your face, Susanna.'

'Thanks a lot, Mel,' I say. 'I didn't notice that new zit on my chin this morning.'

'Look into your *eyes*,' she says, impatiently.

'Okay. I'm looking.'

'Good. Now tell me one thing – is this the face of a girl who lets a boy define her?'

'Gee, I've never had the opportunity. It might be fun. I could call myself, *Ben*anna.'

'Stop joking, Susanna,' Amelia says. 'Look in the mirror and tell me if you see the face of a girl who would sacrifice a by-line in *Scene* magazine just to hang out with a guy.'

I look into my eyes. *Deeply.*

'No, I don't,' I say. And I mean it.

'Who do you see?'

I smile. 'I see Susanna Barringer, reporter extraordinaire. The Girl in the Trunk. The girl who gets the story no matter what.'

'Yes!' Amelia says. 'I'm tearing up.'

Laughing, I reply, 'Hang up and get yourself a tissue. I have an article to write.'

With that, my best friend blows me a kiss through the phone and hangs up.

'Go get 'em, Susanna,' I say out loud. Then I text Ben and tell him I'm sorry, but we can't get together until I've launched my crusade for girls to take back their bodies.

I don't even obsessively check for his reply. I just get to work.

TWENTY-THREE

Amazingly, my article practically writes itself. Once The Body Blog got going, it didn't stop. I got posts from girls mostly, but some guys, women and men, too. As far away as England, as close as some friends from school. Except for a few pro-anorexics who called me 'jealous' and suggested I 'lose the 'tude and eat salad,' I'm totally gratified to see that tons of girls feel exactly the same way I do. Why have we let scrawny, chain-smoking, professionally dressed and made-up walking mannequins make us feel fat and ugly? Not to mention celebrities who have personal trainers, private chefs and on-call plastic surgeons! We should have gathered ourselves in a group and sat on them!

My mind flashes on Ben. *He* made me feel beautiful. Then, when he was gone, I felt like the same old me. I was the girl who needed large clothes called into the fashion closet at *Scene.* The brownie eater. Nell's dog-walker, latte-fetcher, cockroach-killer, ego-stroker and all-around butt-kisser. The terminal virgin. Why did I let myself feel that way?

Rising up from my desk chair, I cross my room to the mirror above my dresser. Once again, I stare at my reflection. The first thing I notice is that my hair looks crappy. Then I stop.

'Rewind the tape, Susanna,' I say out loud.

I close my eyes. Inhale.

'Take two,' I say.

This time, when I look at my reflection, I see a girl with fire in her eyes. My fingers trace her determined jawline. Her chin juts forward, her shoulders are on a hanger – straight and tall – and her chest rises and falls with pride. She's not perfect. Yeah, her hair could use a shampoo. And her nose is on the big side. Along with her butt. But there, before me in the mirror, is *me.* The real me. The Girl in the Trunk, on the red carpet, backstage at Fashion Week. I'm the girl who refuses to give up, who always finds a way, and who will never again let someone else define who she *should* be. Tears rise in my eyes.

'Hi there,' I say. In the bright light of my bedroom, I see the self I'll carry with me for the rest of my life. And the person I see is *beautiful*.

TWENTY-FOUR

Nell scheduled a staff meeting – after school – so I could attend.

'Really?' I said to Nell's assistant, Carmen, when she called to make sure I could be there.

'Seems you are the star of the show,' she said.

Excitement shot through my veins. It had only been three days since I emailed my Body Blog article to her. Was it going to be the cover story? A special feature? Would my article make it into the premiere issue of *Teen Scene* if they ever got around to actually publishing a teen version of *Scene*? Instantly, I had visions of my future as a crusader. I pictured a massive protest in Bryant Park at the next Fashion Week. Led by *moi*. Girls of every size and shape chanting, 'How do we feel? We feel real!'

My heart fluttered. *Wow*, I thought as I hung up the phone, *there really* is *power in the press.*

*

163

As I push through the shiny brass and glass doors into the ground-floor lobby of the *Scene* magazine building, a million emotions flood my consciousness. Excitement and terror are the two biggies. It feels like the first day of school.

'Identification, please,' the guard says to me.

It's the same guard, but he doesn't recognise me. Not that I can blame him. I haven't been through these doors in over a year. He takes my school ID, studies it, then looks up at me.

'Welcome back, Susanna,' he says.

I beam. 'Thanks,' I reply. 'Wish me luck. I'm entering the lion's den today.'

He laughs. 'If Ms Wickham growls at you, never forget that every lion – or lioness – was once a pussycat.'

As the wood-panelled elevator lifts me up to the seventeenth floor, I can't help but grin. How many times had I ridden up to *Scene* magazine feeling petrified, frazzled, hopeful, sweaty, depressed, exhilarated, or – most often – weighted down with an armload of flavoured coffees and low-carb goodies? And now, here I am on the verge of making a giant leap for girlkind!

'Astrid!'

164

The receptionist sneers at me the same way she always did the moment I step off the elevator. Even though I remember to pronounce her name correctly – *Ah*strid, instead of *Ass*trid – the name I called her behind her snotty back.

'You are?' she says.

'Susanna Barringer. Nice to see you. How have you been?'

Astrid's lip curls. 'The intern.'

'That's right,' I say, ignoring the fact that she spits the word 'intern' out like it's sour milk. As Carmen once told me, I can't take Astrid's attitude personally. She's *hungry*.

Hmmm, I wonder, *was it Astrid who logged onto The Body Blog and posted the suggestion that I eat more salads?*

'Nell is expecting me,' I say.

Without looking up, Astrid buzzes me in.

I push the door open, then turn around before I enter the inner sanctum and say, 'You look really great, Astrid.'

For the first time ever, she smiles.

My senses are assaulted the moment I enter the editorial bullpen of *Scene*.

'Fax me the cast bios for the fall line-up!'

'Britney is dating him? Get out!'

'You call this crap coffee?'

Skinny editors dressed in black scurry past me. Heads pop up over the grey partitions and yell updates at each other.

'Viggo Mortensen's nickname is Vig, not Viggie.'

'Jessica Biel's eyes are *hazel.*'

I smell hair gel and perfume, hear a symphony of different ring tones. Suddenly, out of the chaos, Carmen appears.

'Susanna!' She hugs me warmly. Nell's assistant is a calm lagoon in the tsunami of the office.

'How is school?' she asks me. 'Your brothers? Your parents?'

I smile. Carmen remembers that I have a family and a life, while Nell can barely remember my name.

'Everything is good,' I say. 'Maybe even great.'

'Oh my,' she says, walking with me to Nell's office.

'I just may be falling in love,' I say.

'Randall Sanders?'

Now, I laugh. 'No, Carmen. This one is real.'

The major editors are already in Nell's snowball of an office. Renée, the senior celebrity editor, is seated to Nell's right. Her long red curls bounce down her shoulders. Sasha, looking amazing in a chocolate brown mini-dress, waves as I walk in. Keith sits smack in the centre (of course!) of Nell's bright white couch; his faded jeans, black boots and long-sleeved T-shirt hug his body effortlessly. I blush when he winks at me. Then, I instantly beat myself up for being such a doof (nobody said it would be *easy* accepting the real me!).

'Susan!'

Nell rises up on her spiked heels and walks over to me. For a fleeting moment I think she's going to embrace me. My heart definitely skips a beat. By now, I should know better. Carmen takes a seat just as Nell leans close and says, 'You look a bit bloated, Sue. Want a diuretic?'

I laugh. 'No thanks,' I say. 'I'm enjoying the extra hydration.'

Having very close to a bonafide boyfriend, writing an awesome article for *Scene* magazine and starring in a staff meeting instead of catering it, has made me positively giddy.

Boldly, I sit on the couch *this* close to Keith Franklin and wait for the meeting to begin. Behind me, assistants and their assistants shuffle in and stand at the back of the large room. Soon, the entire white room is filled with staffers in black. Except for *moi*. In a conscious effort to dress like myself, I'm wearing beige Gap trousers and a matching ribbed pull-over sweater. And my platform pumps, of course. Which I've come to love.

'Okay, people,' Nell says, 'I'm off to another benefit tonight to save something or cure something or build something in Africa so I don't have a lot of time.'

All eyes face front. Nell runs her hand down her throat and crosses her mega-toned legs.

'I've called this meeting of the entire staff because we are about to witness a rare event.'

Keith leans over and whispers, 'Speaking of rare events, did you ever pick up where you left off?'

I grin and nod. And blush, of course. What a doof.

Nell says, 'Magazine publishing, as we all know, is a game of cat and mouse. We are the cats—'

'Meow,' Bennett, Renée's assistant, says, purring. I chuckle and think, *And you, Nell, were once a pussycat.*

'The *story* is the mouse,' Nell continues. 'Unfortunately, we're competing with all the other cats in town. Often, for one piddly mouse. Usually, the best we can do is share the mouse. But, not today. This afternoon, I brought you all here to present an example of a real catch.'

My heart is now beating double-time. Is Nell talking about *my* article?

'Susie?' she says, startling me.

'Yes?'

'Could you stand please?'

'Stand?'

'Yes. As in rising to your feet.'

As gracefully as I can manage – which is about as nimble as an elephant lumbering out of a mud-hole – I extract myself from Nell's puffy white couch. Suddenly, I feel as bloated as I, apparently, look. And, in the interest of full disclosure, the real me is screeching inside my head, 'What were you thinking?! Beige Gap?' Standing in front of Keith and Sasha and Nell and a staff full of true fashionistas is testing my newly-minted self-acceptance. Honestly, at this moment I would give anything to be draped in black. Or grey, which is the new black. Or is pink the new grey? Like I said, nobody said being me would be easy.

Nell flags me over and hands me two sheets of paper.

'This is what I'm talking about,' she says. 'Susanna?'

'Yes?'

'The floor is yours.'

A print-out of the Body Blog article I emailed Nell is gripped in my hands. 'You want me to read it ... aloud?' I ask.

She rolls her eyes. 'If you read it to yourself, Sue, we'll have to read your *mind*.'

The staff titters. I swallow. My former giddiness is now a lump in my throat. Is this a trap? Am I the mouse? Nell did say she wanted to show an example of a catch. That's good, right? And she did call me Susanna, though briefly. That's a positive sign, right?

'We're waiting,' Nell announces.

'Yeah, okay.' I clear my throat and begin. 'Fashion Week Undressed, by Susanna Barringer.'

Go get 'em, I say to myself. *Meow!*

'It's the fashion event of the year,' I read, my voice shaky. 'A designer's debutante ball. The place to see and be seen by the entire world. But, what this reporter saw backstage – and back home – rips an ugly hole in the very fabric of Fashion Week.'

I glance up, make sure the staff caught my metaphor. Keith nods encouragement. I take a deep breath and continue.

'Chain-smoking, emaciated models who look like

coat racks are no scoop. Everyone knows that the catwalks are crawling with genetic misfits who are too tall and too thin to even appear on the height/weight charts. Except, of course, the *male* models who are simply too beautiful to be real.'

Sasha laughs. Nell says, 'Shhh.'

'The real question is,' I continue reading, 'who is it all for? Me? You? Not likely.

'First, a reality check: a typical American woman weighs one hundred and sixty-three pounds and is under five-foot-four. The average British woman is the same height, but weighs one forty-seven or ten and a half stones. But, get this: the average catwalker is five-foot-nine and one hundred and fifteen pounds. Even after Madrid's ban on super-skinny models during their Fashion Week, models don't even come *close* to looking like regular girls. In fact, the word *model* – defined as "a standard or example for imitation or comparison" – is a joke.'

I pause for emphasis. The room is eerily silent. They're riveted! That giddy feeling creeps back in.

'While it's true many Americans are too fat,' I continue reading, 'why is the "model" body too thin? Is that what girls are *supposed* to strive for? Legs that look

171

like arms, arms that look like skin-covered bones? Are girls supposed to look like boys? Are boys supposed to spend their lives doing sit-ups?'

Now Keith laughs. Bennett says, 'Crunches, actually.'

'Shhh,' Nell repeats.

'After a week in the Bryant Park tents,' I read, 'this teen reporter had one question: why *don't* designers design clothes that real girls with real bodies can wear? When you strip away the spectacle of Fashion Week, what's *really* going on underneath? I went online to find out.'

As I turn to the second page, I notice that the loudest sound in the room is the crinkling of my paper. All eyes are on me. Nobody says a word.

I swallow. Inhale. Read on.

'Here, from The Body Blog – set up to find out how real people really feel about high fashion – are actual postings that give us a peek inside the world's dressing rooms. Fair warning: it's not a pretty sight.

- Girls are suckers! A fashion designer decrees that mini-skirts are back and they blindly buy into it!
- It's all about money, pure and simple. If girls liked

their bodies, they wouldn't spend a gazillion dollars on diets. Wake up! The *goal* is to make you feel fat and ugly.

- A Prada canvas bag costs seventeen hundred dollars. Three hundred million Africans live on less than a dollar a day. The devil doesn't wear Prada; an *idiot* does.

- Designers *can't* design for real bodies! Did you see season three of *Project Runway*? Jeffrey's dress for Angela's mom was hideous. And he *won*!

- Styles change every season for only one reason: to fuel the Capitalist machine and make designers rich.

- What does being a size zero say about you? You're nobody. You don't exist.

- Get a grip, people! We're all being manipulated. Anyone who thinks they need new clothes each season to be cool, is a fool.

- Think about it . . . who would suffer if girls just said no? If we said we're okay having a little junk in the trunk? If we all stood up and said we'd rather be healthy than starved? Why don't we find out????

'Why don't we?' I continue reading. 'To put it bluntly, most girls are mad as hell and they don't want to take it any more. Boys, too. We're enslaved by the struggle to have a six-pack or squeeze into a toddler size. Isn't it time we all broke free? Are you ready to take back your body? To force fashion designers to get real? If so, log onto The Body Blog and let your voice be heard. *Scene* magazine is listening.'

I lower the paper and look out at the sea of faces staring back at me. The hopeful look in my eyes is quickly smothered by the freakish silence in the room. No one says a word. Not one peep. They all just stare, stunned. I'm mortified. Until Nell erupts in applause.

'Bravo, Susie-Q!' she chirps.

Bravo? Wahoo! My heart leaps into my throat. The rest of the staff now starts clapping. Me, I grin uncontrollably, nearly burst into tears. They love me! They really love me! The *real* me – Susanna Barringer, high-schooler, virgin, blogger, trailblazer, Nell's former toady, *Scene*'s future star reporter, the girl who gets the story no matter *what.* Biting my lip, I glance at Keith. *Thank you*, I silently mouth. If not for Keith, I never would have had the guts to tell it like it is.

'I . . . I . . . I don't know what to say,' I stammer, facing Nell. 'Thank you *so* much. I can't tell you how happy I am to get my article published in *Scene.*'

Nell howls. 'Have you gone mental, Anna?'

The applause abruptly stops.

'It's Susanna, actually,' I squeak, temporarily unable to say anything else.

'Whatever.'

Nell rises and glides over to me. 'You'd have to be insane to think we'd ever *publish* an article like that. Good heavens! We'd lose every advertiser we have!'

'What?'

'You didn't think we'd put that in the magazine, did you, Suze? You can't possibly be that daft.'

I'm confused. I stand there, daftly, with my mouth gaping open. Then, my central nervous system revs up. I feel blood rising to my face. My ears get hot. My jaw clenches. All ten fingers curl around the papers in my hand.

'Why did you make me stand up here, in front of everybody and read this?' I ask, unable to hide the anger in my voice. 'To make me look like a jerk?'

Nell says nothing. If the room was quiet before, it was a marching band compared to the silence that suddenly descends now. I see a ton of white eyeballs. But, I don't care. Something has taken hold of me and I'm off and running at the mouth.

'What did I ever do to you, Nell, other than fetch your skim lattes, praise your puffy lips, pick up your dog's poops and find yellow eyeshadow? Which, by the way, was the previous year's colour but no one had the guts to tell you!'

Someone in the back of the room gasps. I notice that Bennett is holding his open cell in my direction. Taping the scene for YouTube, no doubt.

Good, I think. *It's time the whole world knows who the real Nell Wickham is.*

My chest heaves. My cheeks are on fire. Enough is enough. Since the summer before my sophomore year, I've endured everything Nell has dumped on me. This is the final straw. Fashion Week is over. Nell will never hire me again. What have I got to lose?

'I looked up to you,' I tell Nell, struggling not to cry. 'You were my role-model. The woman I eventually wanted to be. But not any more. I don't want to be mean and spiteful, like you. I don't want to squash the dreams of a girl who's just starting out. If making it to the top means making everyone—'

'Susanna.' Keith interrupts me.

'It's okay, Keith,' I say. 'I know I'm going to be

fired. I just don't want to go out without telling Nell how I really feel.'

Nell raises one perfectly-waxed eyebrow.

'And are you finished?' she asks me, deadpan.

'Not quite,' I say.

Bennett holds his camera-phone higher.

'The last thing I want to say is this . . .' I pause, take a deep breath, hang my shoulders on a hanger. 'I'm leaving *Scene* magazine with my head held high. I always did my best for you, Nell, and I'm proud of that. You can never take that away from me. No matter how hard you try.'

Then, for some insane reason, I add, 'Goodbye and good luck,' and clomp my platform pumps to the door.

'Good Lord,' Nell says, rolling her eyes. 'Carmen, stop her.'

Carmen stands and gently grabs my arm before I reach the exit. My heart is pounding so hard, I'm sure the whole room can hear it.

'Feel better now?' Nell asks, standing behind me.

I don't turn around. If I did, I'm sure I'd erupt in slobbery, snot-filled tears. I just want to go home, lie face-down in my heavenly bed, and sleep until college.

'Susanna?' Nell says, softly.

'Yes?' I squeak, still facing the door.

'Remember what I said at the beginning of this meeting?'

'No.' The beginning of the meeting seems like it was days ago. At this moment, I can barely remember my own name. The staff is still as silent as a white-out blizzard.

'I said we were here to witness a rare event.'

I nod. Now I remember. Who knew the rare event was skewering the intern?

'And we have,' Nell says. 'My staff has seen and heard a reporter tell the God's-honest *truth*.'

I blink. Try to calm my thudding heart long enough to make sure I heard what I just heard. Carmen, her hand still on my arm, tenderly turns me around.

'You've opened my eyes, Susanna,' Nell says to my face. 'Because of you, I've seen the kind of clever work a real reporter can do.'

'You have?'

'In you, I see the ability to think outside the box. To be creative. To get the story no matter what.'

'You do?'

'Learning what can and can't be published in a magazine that relies on advertiser dollars is easy. Catching a mouse with a unique cat is hard. You've done the hard work. Sasha can tweak your story into something publishable.'

I stop myself before saying, 'I have?' and 'She will?' and 'Tweak?' With Carmen on my right, and Nell on my left, I'm led back to the centre of the room. My cheeks are burning, and my beige Gap trousers are slightly bunched up in the thigh. Amazingly, I've never felt more fashionable.

Addressing the staff, Nell says, 'I asked Susan to go to Fashion Week and report on what she saw. Every other reporter saw the latest trends, hottest celebs, newest models. But my Sue saw through it all.'

Her Sue? I sniff.

'That's why I've asked Sue to be our editor-at-large for *Teen Scene* which, I'm proud to announce, will finally be launched at the end of next year.'

'What?' I ask, alarmed.

The staff applauds sporadically. Nell turns to me and notices my befuddled face.

'Oh,' she says casually, 'did I forget to mention it to you?'

'Editor-at-*large*?' I ask. 'Is that like an editor who's bigger than a size twelve?'

Everyone laughs. But, I'm not kidding. I have no idea what just happened right before my eyes.

'It means you'll be on special assignment,' Carmen says quietly to me.

'Special?' I repeat.

'Yes,' says Nell. 'And your first assignment starts this summer. *Teen Scene* will be launched simultaneously in the US and England. So, we're sending you off to London to do a feature called, *An American Teen in London*. Sort of like an American in Paris, only it's London. For a month.'

My mouth falls open again. 'Did you say London? For a month?'

'If it's all right with your parents, of course. My sister lives outside the city and has agreed to put you up and be your surrogate mum. Stop by Human Resources on your way out to discuss a salary.'

'Salary? Mom?!'

Suddenly, I stop.

'Hey, wait a minute,' I say. 'Is this a joke? A cruel, mean, awful joke?'

Nell laughs. 'Would I do that to you, Anna?'

Without warning, the dam breaks. Tears sprout from my eyes. Snot runs from my nose. And I fling both arms around Nell's neck.

'You're the best!' I sob. 'I won't let you down.'

She cocks her other perfectly-waxed eyebrow and peels my arms off her saying, 'Brilliant. Now let me go.'

TWENTY-FIVE

How can anyone listen in World History class when they're in love? Why should I care about international relations when I have a bonafide relation*ship* right here at home?

'... Great Wall of China has been called the "longest cemetery on Earth" because nearly a million workers died building it. And in Manchuria ...'

Blah, blah, blah. My teacher blathers on, oblivious to the fact that all I can focus on is my upcoming date with Ben McDermott.

We meet Friday night at the Virgin Megastore in Times Square. *Très* symbolic since that's where I first ran into him with Mel. This time, I don't freak when I walk under the giant neon sign that reads, 'Virgin'. I know it will happen for me when I'm ready. When the time is right.

'You made it.' Ben flips through the CDs in the new releases section. He's wearing a striped rugby shirt over baggy jeans. His thick reddish brown hair glistens with gel. His cheeks are permanently pink. My heart hits a high note just looking at him.

'Yeah,' I reply. 'I took the bus.'

Standing next to him, I flip through the new releases, too.

'So, what's been going on in your life the past two years?' I ask, chuckling.

He smiles. Shrugs. 'Nothing much. You?'

I smile, too. 'Nothing noteworthy.'

We're both lying, of course. And we both know it. In the past two years, *everything* has happened. Ben moved to Chicago, started a new life, a new school, probably had a girlfriend or two, lived through snowstorms and summers and his parents splitting up. Me, well, I've been through it *all*.

'Hey, I have an idea,' I say.

'Hit me,' Ben says.

'Why don't we pick up where we left off?'

Ben laughs. 'I'm down with that.'

'Want a Rice Krispies treat in the café?' I ask.

'I'm more of a brownie guy.'

'Me, too! I love brownies!'

Ben heads for the escalator. I follow. On the way, he reaches back his hand and takes mine. I catch his fingers. But, it's enough. We're linked. I have no idea if we'll stay that way, grow closer or float apart. Will he wait for me to return from London? Will I really want to hear about his life in Chicago if it includes a love he left behind?

Who knows?

Not me.

Not that I care.

Right now, this moment is magic. My lips are grinning, but my heart is singing. No way am I going to wreck this night with what-ifs.

'So,' I say. 'How's school?'

'It sucks. I have to wear a white shirt and tie.'

'That's cool. I hear white is the new black,' I say.

He laughs. I laugh, too. Neither one of us says anything more for a while. Which, bizarrely, feels right. Together, we step off the escalator and silently walk into our destiny. Whatever that may be.

I can't wait to find out.

Coming soon…

SUSANNA
LOVES LONDON

Goodbye NYC! Hello London! In her biggest adventure to date, Susanna jets off to London to score an international scoop for the new *Teen Scene* magazine and dazzle her boss with her cunning, skill and wit.

Needless to say, in true Susanna style, plans don't always go as, well, *planned*. But *nothing* is going to stop this reporter from getting a great story – not Francesca, her snooty arch-nemesis, not her crush on the boy in the chip shop, and definitely not the fact that the bright lights of London seem very faint from the small Kentish village where she's staying…

9781416901600
£5.99

Susanna Hits Hollywood
9781416901587

Susanna Sees Stars
9781416901570

10